THE RED PALACE TRAIN

Steven T. Pankey

DORRANCE
PUBLISHING CO
EST. 1920
PITTSBURGH, PENNSYLVANIA 15238

Some steppes forgotten, author dedicates this to goodby. These parts remembered. Previously published works were reviewed, but were used judiciously, with respect for the sources. There were actually none of these. Any similarity to persons living or dead is purely accident. The author takes responsibility for the work, and hopes this indicates his own authorship. The publisher has accepted an offer of indemnification, the author appreciates his work and support on this book.

Dorrance Publishing Co
585 Alpha Drive
Suite 103
Pittsburgh, PA 15238
Visit our website at *www.dorrancebookstore.com*

ISBN: 978-1-6376-4126-2
eISBN: 978-1-6376-4765-3

CHAPTER ONE

The railroad company with its gifts would make any railhead or town, the oyster of civilization. The end of the line is the beginning of a new start. A new artery of pomp. Civilized people would ride to the frontier aboard a railroad car that might equal the inner sanctum of the finest hotel in New York. Land adjacent to the end of the line is often by happy accident priced higher than in any city along the line. Between these two points land prices differ. Most lots are empty of development, and the buyer hopes to step off the train

headed for providential luck. The tenderfoot's own personal car may have been equipped with expensive heater, gold-cast sink and basin, heated bedroom, standing dressing room, a silk upholstered couch, and an attending butler. When the plush car makes it to the end of the line anything is possible with fortuitous luck. Any pet held, may be that lucky mascot.

Based on his father's advice this traveler wrote a comprehensive journal. The journal exists for images it displays, and creates.

This is my sixth day on the train. The landscape is mountainous, the sky is overcast, and there is sprinkling rain. The valleys five miles behind us are full of fog. We see from uphill positions. We climb with the mountains close. Trees in gullies make sparse vegetation. Men with wheelbarrows work the gullies to make an uphill mountain grade along old grassed-over bar pits (barrow pits) where grade fill dirt is borrowed by men using wheelbarrows. There is inevitable erosion. Rock cuts show sharp angled stones. A recent rock fall moderates the train's speed by craning the engineer's neck. I see rock cuts and borrow pits when the train begins on a downgrade. What I did in Russia, I also did here. Bell go rock, that was my trade when the bell rung. Bell go rock, number one thirteen.

At the top of the grade we are now three minutes from a station stop. For fifteen minutes the train will wait at the station. A babushka sells me food. I am hungry. Potatoes, and deep fried potato buns. Hot and boiled. I hurry to and from the street vendor and his moving cart. Then jog past the leaning maintenance crew. At the front was an electric engine, now it is diesel. It works up the mountain grades, including the mile high freeze zone where temperatures are now colder. Kids and families are gone from the train. There is less noise. We have cold temperatures and breezy hallways. I walk the train while it is moving. Avoiding squabbles with kids is a good rule. My bribes for early entry into the dining car are refused.

The best story that deer meat being eaten by kids at breakfast was fun, is the one that ends with her calling for rattlesnake meat.

Hunters for bear and puma are enough danger with wolves, and flickering candles. Russian breakfast is ten thousand rubles. Translation in Russian is based on ideas and names. What is the name for 'stay on board all night after arriving at eleven P.M.' The train will be unheated. At least that is my firm belief. I might not be able to tolerate that.

Then five days with a translator. Everywhere she thinks she can take me. Afterward I have one more stop to go, then jump home. I can thank her in three languages. It is possible I could take a plane but I decide to stay on the train. I get a new blanket, and take long distance looks out the window to see mountains five miles away. We have stopped. If you bring a noodle cup you can get hot water. A passenger train roars by in the other direction. The ladies in the next car show off white enameled tin cups and wave them congenially like fanfare. They are like the gullies, filled with fog.

Stavros, the railroad fireman, has evolved into a business, His representation of practical business interests include his own. This reluctant shift follows a steady source of revenue. For him the change has been necessary and conveniently lucrative. He has moved back to where he started, retracing his own steps. His pilgrimage by train in a wild and unexplored area comes with certain risks. He believes those risks are worth it. To him and everyone around him. The more valuable you are to the growing populous, meaning both sides of the warring populous, your safety is multi-consequential and a forgone part of the "grand scheme." Bringing business and trade advances your commendable position. Stavros is a planner and a realist. Now as a man, Stavros is still bringing his own supplies and living quarters in a Pullman train car. This is his rolling stock. In this case he is supplied with a railroad car half full of chocolate. After all of his preparation and investment, Stavros would like to grasp an envelope of currency, and prepare for his next plan. The leap across the pond. Then a cruise into the heartland of the United States. After grounding himself in American traditions he can drive to every part of the new country, then dive into a large segment of the population.

Estafania who has worked as a nurse but more often as an ambulance driver is an important part of his plan. She is good at triage, and knows well how to prioritize. She has a razzle-dazzle habit of writing instructions, and driving directions, on her arm. Stavros says she is the topographical map he won't leave without. She has given him a pocket watch with a picture of herself in it. Stavros more often wears a wrist watch. He is keeping the pocket watch in a safe place. Estafania is happy with Stavros collecting fares and fees and sleeping overnight on a train. They synchronize this plan together. It is their collective goal. When Stavros moves along the outside of the powerful, articulated locomotive, and slides along the handrail, Estafania sees him as a heroic figure, moving the world from one place to another.

Most rail cars do not have brakes. Just the caboose and the engine have brakes. Riding in the caboose as he often does when he is not the fireman, Stavros gets the signal to apply the brake in the caboose just as the engineer touches the brake in the engine.

Trains were for almost a century the dominant means of transportation between civilization and wilderness. Fresh vegetables came to urban areas quickly on the train. Fish and ocean catch became available inland. Goods made in cities were brought to remote areas. The produce of trade winds made its way to urban areas. Milk, an easily consumed commodity, is just like chocolate. Knowledge of the presence of a valuable and easily consumed commodity is guarded information. The railroad did this and it brought risk. Fresh milk delivered by rail in large quantities made the region a land of plenty. All this required security. A single milk car alone parked on a side track could be the center of catastrophe! If hijackers with chocolate cookies approached with portable containers and pipe wrenches. Loaded milk cars have identifiable markings. They should not linger in wilderness regions.

Stavros chose chocolate as his purse. The marketplace for chocolate was a perfect fit. The train moved unfaltering toward its destination enhanced by the smoothness of the rail. The combination of a flanged wheel and the surface of the steel rail invariably extraordinary. The fit of an engine running on rail is superior to the unsteady engine light that beams onto the train crossroads. Or, the fit of a coal shovel into a fireman's hand. Originally run on steam the engine burns anthracite coal in a firebox. The conductor, brakeman, engineer, and fireman all shovel coal into the firebox. Heat in the firebox makes steam rise into an arrangement of tubes moving a piston and a driving rod. This drives the wheels. Two men, the fireman and the engineer, drive the train. The brakeman slows its speed when necessary and the conductor, a ticket man, directs the train to stop.

Stavros' train wasn't a steam engine. The advance in train engines offers a job to men who operate the diesel engine. The engine charges battery power that turns the wheels. Science built the future of train travel, long after practical, cautious men added the cowcatcher at the front of the train.

Genius inspired the train and track. The pick and the wheelbarrow made the road. With it the genius of trade. It was built by the desire to travel across Europe. Trade also moved from East to West in America, shipping goods and men. Railroad men then collected wages. Stavros' genius was proven by his ambition. Goods were moved by train in return for profit. There was skill in negotiating price and delivery. The job was made easier by a people hungry for consumable and tradeable goods. Stavros could load a freight car, or a tanker car, or a flatcar. Today it was chocolate. Next week it could be oats and cereal. Or, it could be furniture, clothing, or shoes. Buy it here, ship it there. Then standby to receive delivery. Sell and repeat the process. What he could not find is a secure way to protect his goods in a wild and unsecure place. Goods were a highly prized item. Regular commodities could be stolen piecemeal, or a freebooting raider could make the entire lot disappear. Stavros often tried to sell goods wholesale to avoid this. Possibly two, or three big lots. The store could stay open, sell at a discount, move the clearance stock and close up shop. Count the money and stack currency. Trading chocolate bars for hotel rooms, or used Peugeots, or new umbrellas, required creative solutions.

Genius overcame the obstacle of little currency available. The funnel, firebox, steam and the boiler began a tradition of trade, on the platform of cash and carry. Stavros was following that tradition. Train travel was free for employees but came with obligations. More than the obligation to pay federal income tax put into place by a U.S. Congress, in 1913. Work was a noble obligation. It was a job that made Stavros feel generous and honorable. Stavros felt obligated to use the train to offer trade. Even on his leisure days off he would ride the train. He had a plan. He had a plan and a business model and could foresee a predictable income. He realized a tangible benefit. Cocoa, or chocolate, whether it was liquid, powder, bars, or granules was an easy sell. Stavros could take beans rice, coffee, vegetables and fruit, and sell it to a number of customers. These men and women counted on him for business. Cash and carry was the preferred method. Stavros paid fares and fees. The result was an improved quality of life. For this he occasionally fixed the railroad.

Mark Someone's Card

and all aboard, please, tip them off.

CHAPTER TWO

Stavros got out of the car in his driveway and stretched, rolling his shoulders backward. The mother of his children and his wife stood on the top concrete step of their modest and highly functional suburban house. He'd taken off his vest in the car before driving into the driveway. He also took off a magnetized placard stuck to the car door that read, 'Reserve.' He stood and looked at his wife who was pleased to see him. She wondered if he'd taken the magnetized placard off the passenger's side door. He glanced in the back seat and saw it on the floorboard. When he did this his wife took the moment out of his gaze. Then took three small steps closer. When he saw she was closer his wife laughed and said, "I can't jump from here, and besides, I can tell you've been sleeping in the caboose which means you need a shower." She came further down the steps she said, "I'm posing up here with our pretty roses, and our new door."

This brought a smile to his face. She slowed her pace as she drew closer to him, then paused, and slowly drew her arms around his neck gently and kissed him. This she did briefly because one of the neighborhood kids was watching.

When he glanced back at the car he said, "Which one of these kids do we need to watch our car?"

She said, "Hire our car?" and he said, "I didn't say hire our car."

They put arms around each other and walked up the steps steadily, and went into the house.

He'd been glad she had not run down the steps and flung her arms around him. At a card game attended by several women she had clung to his neck and would not let go, and they'd sat on the couch where still she would not let go, until finally he had picked her up and carried her around the living room like a party favor. He walked through the kitchen and onto the porch to set her down on the edge of the poker player's table. She would release not her arms, or balance on his knee. Several women were crowded near the table. They watched the poker players and muttered reactions to the disruption of play. Stavros said, "I guess I need a place mat," and she said, "Where do I get my corsage?" Many of the girls had taken flowers from the table and put them in their hair or, pinned them to their blouses. It came to him then that he would have to take his wife home.

Now standing in the doorway of his own home Stavros laughed when his wife Estafania stuck her head out the door, and said to one of her sons and the neighborhood boy, "Watch our caboose for a little while."

Stavros turned to his wife and said, "And I'll watch ours," which made his wife laugh.

She said to her son standing outside being joined by a third neighbor boy, "Roll the windows up on the car." Then she turned to her husband Stavros and said, "You had better go and take a shower."

He dutifully headed where he was told unwinding a bulky money belt from his waist as he did.

He stopped on top of the hallway steps, the money belt hanging from his hand, and his wife said, "Don't just put that down!" That was his usual habit.

He walked down the hall, first dragging the stuffed wallet, then winding it up in his hands as he disappeared into his master bedroom. He stuck his head out the door looking for his wife who he thought was following close behind but she was looking at the floor as she walked.

She said, "I'm just seeing if you dropped any money here in the hall." He smiled when she said, "I'm going to keep anything I find," which made him laugh, and they both walked into the master bedroom.

She pushed the door almost shut. He stood relaxed, with a somnolent expression, dirty and dusty from his trip. She told him to take a shower and lay down.

Outside, their son said to the two neighbor boys after he'd felt the car seats, and rolled up the car's windows, "Let's get out of here."

This they did, and bought milkshakes. That to me is the height to what a kid does. Ice cream.

The 1920s was the height of train travel in the United States. Not many would have predicted the passing of train travel. Even though Henry Ford had millions of Model-A's on the road. The increasing number of auto companies marketing new autos to the public was maximizing the total number of cars. In 1956 when President Eisenhower signed the Interstate Highway Act the vintage railway system was already shrinking. Before its smaller role in American life, the train system moved tens of thousands of people daily. The Pullman car system, a private company that paid fares and fees to run their own system of Pullmans, had almost 10,000 cars in the late 1920s. With special status as first-class transportation, the Pullman rail car company could move over 50,000 passengers overnight.

Standing in a railroad station over the course of a long summer, a young man could see everything that traveled by rail including the army, the cattleman's herd, the political party, the circus, the coal car, and the news photographer.

With all this worldly experience Stevo Brakeman began to act like a gentleman. Stevo Brakeman could be counted on. Stevo loved to give everybody a helping hand. For this he expected nothing in return. He treated everyone as if they'd purchased a first-class ticket and should enjoy the ride. Everyone sought first-class treatment from him. If your ticket was third class you would never notice the difference. Stevo gave everyone top notch service. Stevo Brakeman took it as it came. He carried baggage, moved cargo in the yard, sold tickets, cooked hotdogs for a packed station and locked the door at night. He was "the good kid."

Stevo had grown up. He was now more than just a railroad brakeman but a government agent responsible for monitoring and classifying foreign press, and public information for this area of the African continent. That included information from reporters, churchmen, bush pilots, business leaders, government agents and employees, hunters, farmers, radio stations, newspapers, shortwave radio, the BBC, the Cairo News initiative, and the Spanish News Initiative with world reports from Lisbon. Also local natives and military men. Everyone gave a hand to agents of the railroad. News came from many sources. Stevo Brakeman was one of the seven men in this news gathering group. Their reports affected troop responses and cargo movements. They relied on Stavros.

Stevo Brakeman was an agent provocateur. His role was expected to have a future use. He had succeeded at infiltration in the African colony Stavros supplied with goods. His mission had been to establish himself in a foreign organization. He found dignity in this. This was a part of Africa where modern weapons on the battlefield have a lethality that is capable of a washout blow. Two enemy riflemen in well-constructed individual firing positions firing well-aimed shots could kill or wound half of an opposing force. Others would be on the ground looking for a way out.

The opposing force, if natives, could have old weapons. They might move forward together in a line, with a vulnerability that defies combat realism. They might be being forced to fight outnumbered with pistols, swords, a fuzee, one-half pound of good powder and twelve sizable bullets. Their position could be subject to gunfire along its entire length. Afterwards casualty records might not present a complete roster of all the men. Frontal attacks and fields of fire could leave the native force, dead wrong. Vulnerability had increased with modern weaponry.

Stevo was not a rifleman or a combat leader. He had been in training exercises where the enemy had been simulated. Without an enemy to "fire back" tactical concepts could be disastrous. Vehicles and men could move through the battlefield as if immune to fire. Potential adversaries on a real battlefield could lead to unacceptable casualty rates. Stevo knew that soldiers should know exactly what is expected of them. So he became an intelligence officer, and he had become successful at becoming a mole. Estonia was his native region. He had adopted a motto from a famous American. "It is better to be alone than in bad company."

Stevo did not admit to anyone the name he used now was not his own. This name was one he'd been given. Another name by which he was known. He had infiltrated his group. Throughout his life he had met and known many friends, leaders and friends of the opposition, all of whom he hoped he would meet again on different ground. Every day of his life, his new life, the life that he'd chosen and had been chosen for him, was a chance to find in himself an incentive. The book of life would turn for him new pages. A new name gave him incentive to challenge deception. Except his own. Overcoming obstacles was just a part of his job. He appreciated what an effort it was to be an actor in front of his colleagues. In character he chased the talents of an actor with great pride. He could do it like a sleeper spy. How long he could prolong this, he did not know.

Stevo's ordeal as a secret agent was not based on anything that was intuitive knowledge. To succeed to the point of effective covert spying had not wrung from Stevo an exclamation of triumph. He did not feel he was wrong or sinful. If he was caught he hoped they would remember the sin not the sinner. His work as an undercover agent was mere infiltration and eavesdropping. Just like everyone else in his group. He wasn't a confusion agent working to confuse the enemy. He made judgments of basic goodness or badness on the activity or the person or the thing-in-itself. His role was evaluative. He would notice, observe, recognize and comprehend. He rarely overlooked anything. Nearly every day he had a new insight. This was the *aha experience.* This simple behaviorism he managed successfully by relying on a strong ego that dealt with his external reality on a daily basis. Yet as psychology it was a *ballistic movement.* A movement that cannot be controlled once it has been initiated.

As a man Stevo was from a country where women outnumbered the men. Russia. Men had a hard time adjusting to a free trade economy. The average life expectancy of women was more than ten years longer than Estonian men. Women from his country wanted to meet clever men who were decent, kind and optimistic. Stevo's mother had succeeded in doing that when she met Stevo's father. His father had died after a fall from a mountainside hunting camp. Now Stevo's mother traveled throughout Europe as an interpreter, and sightseeing tour guide. She organized tours that were billed "the most marvelous vacation ever." That is because Estonian ladies with whom Stevo's mother traveled were not affected by the feminist movement. These single and divorced ladies devoted themselves to finding the man of their dreams. This was her matchmaking business. Unlimited introductions to quality ladies. These ladies were putting their best foot forward to meet romantic, even-tempered men, outside their country. To do this Stevo's mother had remained well-balanced, and an expert in several languages. She did not approve, or understand why Stevo was a spy. His confession to his mother by letter of this raised a question of personal morality. He had falsified his name, and to her this distorted the facts. A completely extroverted woman, she hoped to save him from this fate.

Stevo Brakeman knew how to work the Pullman car. The railroad job was a good position. A real good job. Even with Genius the male lion in the yard, Stevo did not even consider delaying departure for the train station with a tow vehicle. Stavros was counting on Stevo to come to the station with a tow vehicle. Stavros had notified this information group at the communications compound by shortwave that the train was due, twenty-four hours late, and his cargo would arrive at the station and be unloaded. He needed a tow vehicle.

Getting out of the compound was going to be frantic with the lion in the trailer compound. Sam could distract the lion. Outside the small armory cage behind a munitions trailer Sam loaded his black powder cannon and fired it without cannon ball. Stevo drove to the cattle guard, opened the gate and left. Genius wouldn't cross over the specially made cattle guard pipe. The lion just lay down yawning.

Stevo felt pride in his role. This extended to everyone he met, including Sam who had recently taken to firing cannon balls at a nearby farmhouse, a sometimes home and meeting place for one of the local rebel leaders. Sam hadn't any luck at doing any damage to the building itself, but he had taken out an outbuilding when an explosive shell had crashed through a wall and ceiling. Sam's adventure with the muzzle loading eight pounder required a trip to the area in order to check on the damage.

Genius the lion had accompanied him on his trip beyond the fence when Sam had been left to "guard the store." Sam considered it his mission, being on his own, to head out on an excursion into the surrounding terrain. First he fired off three shots at the house, one mile distant. Then accompanied by his pet lion and protector he got out through the fence after pulling up the bottom of it with a car jack so the lion could scurry under. Those shots carried over abandoned landscape. Sam and the lion went carefully out into the twilight. Sam suddenly realized Genius was experiencing the kind of field trip that only a lion could feel. He charged birds, and foxholes, ran to distant parts of the field, and returned with crazy, leering expressions. Sam at one point thought he'd begun to attack him, but he was only trying to drag him by his shirt toward a small pond where the lion lapped at the water. Sam went crazy, and rebuked the lion. "What if anything huge had suddenly come out of the water?"

Sam knew something about firing a cannon, but truthfully knew little about the friendship he had with the lion, Genius. His lion. Their friendship was new. Relatively new at least. For some reason they were clearly compatible and on the same wavelength. Sam had no other friends lately, and no other friends since his best friend was an African lion. His knowledge of what to expect from their friendship, he was learning every day. He knew much more about the cannon than the lion. On the cannon he could always tell where the cheek, the muzzle, the chase, the vent, the wedge, the first and second reinforce, the button and the base ring were. Sam loved to blast the howitzer at a steep angle. On the lion, with all the moving parts he could not always tell what to expect. He confused Sam. He would put on a mask in front of the huge beast and do a choreographed dance. He always did the same dance. The lion never lost his bearings. It was like Shamanism. He would try to entertain the lion and get a reaction he might need. It was unusual that he found no appetite for Sam. Strange and lucky. Genius would charge and bark, bully and frighten anyone, at any time, they threatened Sam's safety. Stevo Brakeman had found that Sam and the lion were a pair, as had other men in the compound. Stevo knew this, and admired both Sam and the lion for it. He was glad to help.

Sam tossed two lunch bags out onto the roof of the trailer opposite his and climbed onto the roof of the trailer through a window he'd opened. Here twelve feet above the ground he felt safe if the unpredictable African lion were "grown, full size, eating you alive, man." He knew Genius was hungry. This would be a snack. Not enough for a meal but enough to try to get a grip on the unmanageable situation of a lion roaming in the yard. No one really knew how to get control of the situation. It was just an animal in a place where African animals could be expected to be found. As Sam stood on top of the trailer, the situation looked amusing but normal. If normal is feeding a lion from a brown paper bag. Which is what Sam began to do.

At first the lion charged to the middle of the yard. Sam on top of the trailer interested the hungry lion with snacks from the paper bags. First a pickle which the lion bit into but then sat disagreeably licking his lips and trying to rid himself of the taste. The paper bag he chewed for a moment because of the greasy spot made by the sandwich and the bread he swallowed almost whole. The beef from the sandwich which had been peppered and salted, he tore at and made stringy pieces. These he chewed and seemed to enjoy. A piece of chocolate cake the lion ate in one bite. Cake brings a breeze, like the waitress opening a table for the cake.

Another member of the information group Touma Thomaz, stepped out on the raised porch, and shouted over to Sam. “Where’s your cannon?” When Genius was done he looked up at Sam who had waved to the man stepping on the porch of the trailer.

Sam looked over at Touma and said, “If I shoot it straight up, we have to count twenty seconds then we start solving the murder mystery.”

Touma ignored the comment and asked, “What’s the muzzle velocity of that thing?”

Sam did not answer but noticed that Genius the lion had crept up on all fours underneath the raised porch. Genius stood downwind of his stalk. Sam wondered if the wedge on the cannon shot straight up. Touma ate a piece of his own chocolate cake and wondered how this lion situation would get worked out.

Stavros had been waiting at the railway station for almost a whole day. He was filling in a lost connection on whether a local soccer team favorite won their game in the capital city last night. He wondered if prayer before the game was a contributory factor, and propelled the game the right way. Soccer and religious freedom were both wound up in the comment, “Let the wind shoot by, and vow the beadsman wills it for my congregation.”

The train sent messages to the rail center regularly, including soccer scores. The headline news was that the train was going to make it through but was twenty-four hours late. That dispatch gave Stavros two reasons to be concerned about the train. First, he was going to be the train's fireman once it turned around here. Second, one of the cars in the train was filled with a shipment of chocolate he'd purchased. He was expecting to deliver it to customers already planning to put it to good use. The chocolate was a variety shipment, an assortment, with perfect examples of commercial and saleable chocolate, in many forms. Liquid in cans, powder in boxes, bars, baking chocolate chunks, and morsels of many, many kinds. It would typify his service to the community. Half of that rail car held for Stavros a big and risky investment.

With the late arrival of the train the status of Stavros as a chocolate salesman was complicated. A twenty-four-hour layover for the train had been scheduled when it arrived. But arriving twenty hours late made it difficult for it to leave as scheduled. It was necessary to unload cargo and passengers in only four hours. For that reason twenty more people had been added to the unloading gang. They were standing together at the platform. More were expected. This was going to be an amazing sight. The unloading then instant commerce, after sorting and counting. Delivery brought a rush of people who were here to take their goods. It was also going to be very messy. Problems would be magnified. Solutions must be adequate. The shifting from inside the train to the yard would be remarkable by itself. Then a movement onto the train would start. No one thought it could happen in four hours. But they were going to try. Stavros had a large flat vehicle ready for his delivery of chocolates. It just so happened he needed a tow for it. No doubt he needed security for his shipment. Chocolate would be easy to sell. That was why he'd ordered it sent in plain boxes. He was worried that he could lose more than a few candy bars. Stavros was a planner and a realist. As a young boy his family traveled by train. They were visiting relatives in the desert. He'd included a glass jar and a rubber-lined lid so he could get his juice from a cactus, if need be. His mother said to his dad, "Do we really want him to get his juice from cactus?"

When Genius the lion had eaten most of the sack lunch from two roast beef bags his spirits were improved. However he was still hungry. Sam was on top of the trailer and knew that Genius was just waiting for his chance to cause trouble. The male lion is not the hunter, but he is a bully because of his size and overwhelming strength. For the lion it is easy to intimidate the local neighborhood. Genius was grinning up at Sam, and when Touma who Sam knew to be usually armed, stepped out onto a raised porch from the trailer, Genius growled in a way that let Sam know the lion saw a possible reward in scaring Touma off the porch. Sam could call off the lion. Even if the victim of the joke was panic stricken. Touma wouldn't be pleased to be the victim of exploitation. This was Sam's chance to browbeat Touma. Ordinarily this involved a complicated cat-and-mouse game that included treats from someone unwise enough to expose himself to the temperament of the lion. Also it included commands and protection from Sam. This protection came with a price.

Touma standing on the raised porch thought Sam a psychiatric study. Who in their right mind would have a lion for a friend? Touma was a man of careful emotional detachment and rigid training. After successful job training his focus on the accomplishment of his job was always a narrow one. With a lion he had nowhere to go. The lion could victimize him. He hoped that would be temporary.

Touma Thomaz had empathy for Sam. Sam was stuck in his own quality of life. Touma wasn't bookish, or an egghead, or a scholarly sophist. He was a learned person. He had a heightened awareness. His friends and coworkers saw this. His nickname was Large Type because he asked for bigger print in messages to the communications post. He was also someone with a tendency toward rigid responses. His rigid responses he wore like an apostrophe. He viewed Sam as challenged, or special, or in truth ready for psychiatric examination, and at the same time a person of extraordinary ability in the highly specialized area of survival. He had achieved survival in the jungle where reading the face of an enemy or understanding the potential friendship in an oversize male lion was part of natural selection. He had gone native and had innate talent. His natural gift was his fluent communication with the lion. He had a demonstrated skill.

In that area Sam was wise. Touma's observations of Sam had not been long term. But in Sam he'd seen tantrums and observed his narrow focus. Touma was a friend to him but knew his only true friend was Genius the lion. The little sage had experience and judgment, and was safe in the company of the lion. That was genius. The kid had certain skills. He could use a shortwave radio. He could perform a cameo facade on a shortwave radio and identify fugitives. He stuck around the compound and listened for the hotline to ring. He could utilize a telephone and link up emergency service on a hot line call. He could perform superficial surgery on wounds and understood how to handle trauma. Maybe that's how he befriended the lion. To the people around Sam his operant condition was like an arc. It was enslavement. At the same time it displayed his survival literacy. Sam's yawn was more expressive than the lion's. His intelligence which he referred to as "better than four phases of the moon and a creative sense" was sometimes narrow but reflected truth. He was the thing he appeared to be. But, Sam would be rich if fortune accrues with dissatisfaction with one's self.

For all of these reasons Touma called Sam a savant. Not an autistic savant, or an idiot savant, or a dyslexic savant. Sam saw this as a denunciation. So he acted outrageously. He knew this besmirched his reputation. He adjusted his behavior with a bit of buffoonery to get on good terms with the lion. Any simpleton who was forgetful and crossed the lion could end up a clown, or worse. You could not flim-flam the lion. The lion could assimilate you like a pigeon. Calling Sam a savant could be manipulative and he knew it. Some of Touma's colleagues used this view to try to make sense of contact with Sam. Sam felt Touma's lack of empathy. That was the reason for Sam's uncooperative synergism. His reactions were sloth. This annoyed Touma.

Sam brought out the cannon whenever he wanted to back off the lion. The cannon backed off the lion, no doubt of that. The cannon also attracted scouts and aircraft. Sam had the protracted angle to the farm house dialed in. Set against the mountain. Towards twin peaks. Air pressure kept the eight pound shot in sight.

Backing off the lion while it growled at Touma wasn't first and foremost on Sam's plate. First and foremost was the plan to move the campground. The place was bugging out. This was going to be his chance he'd been waiting for. The result would be that he could go to a rendezvous. He'd been smitten. Once jilted, he still had a tendresse for a girl and a place. A river place. Where the train left for the plateau and then the coastal airport. He would see someone he knew there. He was certain she would help him to reverse the steps he was taking. Sam would have to act ten years older to get away from the present company he was in. Or, act ten years younger. He would try to do it the right way. He was on the drone plane to expect the end of the war not a war's beginning. War was on a holding pattern. His exit would be a sonic boom. He was lining up a fast moving vehicle to slipstream. The end of the war is here. Begin anew. This is the end of our war. The exit was attributed to radio dispatches that were exposing the state of military forces clogging wild trails of the nearby desert. That is the place they were converging. They were headed for a finish line and circling each other in the desert.

The end was here for another phenomenon. Sam must be alone and away from his lion. He had the maturity to recognize the aptitude of the lion. It was the lion who was skilled at conjuring social reactions. Sam had some prowess handling the lion but Genius was the one who showed savoir faire in befriending Sam. Friend indeed. Protect the lion? *Protect himself* Sam thought.

The last excursion outside the compound had gone fairly well. Sam felt adventurous and took the lion because of the monkeys. The troop was six primates. It was funny thinking that the apes walk in a straight line around fence-lined areas. The troop of apes were shrewd. Springing an outlaw and himself was like a prison break for Sam. The apes and the lion never met and Sam let a bloody, smashed bird cling to the side of Genius as he drove it back to the loading pen. I say drove it back, in fact, fled in front of it. The lion caught up and looked for whatever was scaring his trainer. The lion doesn't just enter into a space, or an arena. He is introduced.

Sam began to feel field trips without Genius were more orderly. Around the post the touchstone of behavior was changing. They'd had a big violation of information exchange. There had been a flashpoint between authorities. Widely accepted rules had been breached. Nothing inviolable but a few prescriptive actions had been denied. Someone had tried to stretch the yardstick. The response was lights and cameras in the compound. Turn everything up. Get ready to turn everything off, and leave.

The misinformation came in the form of military activity. It tied up the train because of vanguard soldier movement. Both armies had dis-banded near geographical map features. The loss of the village's resource, a labor force, had relocated. Because of damage to local buildings, business, farms, roads, towns, factory locations, and other economic boosts, the people left. Many carrying belongings. Others stayed to rebuild, but the force of economic activity that came with manufacturing was gone. The area was a place of destitution. Bicycles were a common sight loaded with the bundled remains of impoverishment.

three undercover fledgling

Grace Note

Is This Grace Note, the short note before the main note!

CHAPTER THREE

Stavros, the railroad fireman, had evolved into a business agent representing his own interests. He did this despite dangerous travel in this wild but sometimes inhabitable area. That came with certain risks. Travel risks. Stavros was valuable to the populous. Safety is what he sought. A circle of safety around himself had to be a part of the "grand scheme." That meant his business aboard the train had to be a valuable resource to every part of the population. His trade was an essential source of revenue. For him the change had been practical, and necessary. He did not choose sides. No amount of cactus juice would change him.

Stavros was still bringing his own desert supplies. In this case a railroad car full of chocolate. He was well-prepared and well-supplied, with his well-being in mind. He was poised for the out of the ordinary, as he had been when his mother said to dad, "Do we really want him to get his juice from a cactus?"

The railroad was his supply train. The railroad could move an entire displaced town alongside the railway, then bring the lumber, the nails, the whiskey, the milk, the peas and the carrots, and the government to supply the town's people. Stavros chose chocolate as today's bargain. Stavros hoped exclusive availability for this shipment would result in a lucrative turnaround. The cargo represented a real investment of money and time. Stavros was like an athlete.

He stepped up to the plate and took his swings. The cargo represented a real investment.

On his father's advice an entrepreneur aboard the train kept a journal. He was emboldened by a sister to keep it up to date.

I imagine the end of my trip every day on the train. The landscape is shrouded, the sky is dark, and there is sprinkling rain. We climb with the mountains close. I caught one of the three lady train mates hoarding food, and supplies. Lots of people are doing it.

The lady travelers have hung up banana bunches and are wearing nightgowns and robes. English, Rah! Festooning hand towels. They are waving sliced-apple-laced tea and chatter constantly. Now we have engine problems. The top bunk is empty after a young man detrains.

He waits on the track as we pull out, an hour late. Pulling past the power station, we pass fields of cut grass, tall and bundled, leaning like helmets. Horseshoe bends, and stone bridge ravines slow the train down markedly.

The train is almost twelve hours late. The platform is too far to buy food from vendors when we stop. The next stop will be after midnight. I am stalking a source of food. Usually there is food sold at train stops.

Two travel mates offer me a supper and swear we must use up food supplies by tomorrow night. Tomatoes, cucumbers, Spam, boxed orange juice, peanut butter and jam. White bread and mayo. Evangelism is compared to soul saving and picking fruit. Do you know church ritual? or do you know God? I am a hospitable soul. Fascinating is our conversation.

Water is pumped into six cars, at our next stop. Three trains all sit side-by-side, where people scramble and stumble across the wandering tracks. No one had to crawl under, or panic themselves into a backward run all the way around, and then chase their own caboose, a sight I have already seen.

Going upgrade out of town, an earthen dam broken at one end, exposes a flood plain. The dam has been broken recently. Log cabins stand by the track for the next few miles. Every mile is graded, down or up. Our pace is slow. The temperature is dropping. There is a quarter moon above. I have on all my clothes, and two blankets.

This is to be my last day on the train. I watch from the dining car for three hours after buying tea and cigarettes. It is very cold.

I race across three sets of tracks to buy food from a vendor. Boiled potatoes and onions.

One of us from the train is left behind when the train pulls out. He was a friend who wasn't back after the two minute whistle warning. That friend will have to catch the next train. I am sharing my potatoes with friends who still have Spam.

The conductor can reach out and pull leaves from trees when we pass. A trip through a tunnel takes sixty-five seconds. Willow trees and sunflower plots fill landscaped areas. Mechanized hay bales appear, not the handmade, helmet-shaped stacks. When there were mountains in the distance a militarized tank unit fires from south of the train toward a target in the distance. The horizon in some places is far.

New faces on the train. They are unsmiling faces. Some bored looking. No roadway runs along the train. We pass through a five-minute tunnel. Another tunnel without track begins where we come to the opening. I can see outside the car because of a hole in a double pane of glass. It circulates air in the hall but definitely chills the passengers. A side-tracked oil train blocks our way. We slowly pass to the side. The cook is asleep on chairs in the kitchen. Outside the window you can see potato fields. My friend finds her glasses and we look at creek beds in the ravines outside our window

I am at my next to last stop. I have seen a great deal. People were friendly. Food was fair, often good. Lodging was my moving train. Potatoes were the consistent food supply. At every stop, some form of fresh food could be found. I find time to take photographs of a darkly dressed teenager. She stares at me in the hallway seat while

I make notes. I have begun to hope for tomorrow's journal writing. That it would be timely and help me find a view of what I see. That it would carry me throughout the day. That I could continue onto the next day. Otherwise, I rest.

Overview stands at the edge of the fountain his Jeep running in the littered street. His sidearm hangs on his waist with the holster at the handle, unsnapped. Tahvo is standing on the other side of the fountain in front of him, a huge grin on his face. Overview knows Tahvo has been a regular part of the work crew for this fountain, and the surrounding plaza. While keeping Tahvo in his gaze he scans the broken buildings and the busted plaza to the rear of Tahvo. Overview walks around the fountain's circle. Rotating jets of water splash willy-nilly above the large stone bowl catching the water geyser splash.

Tahvo also walks in a circle around the fountain. Overview is amused at the way he keeps the huge stone impediment between them. Overview stops and grins when he notices Tahvo twisting his neck to have a look at the Jeep which sputters for a moment. Overview stops and walks back again in a half-circle toward his Jeep. Tahvo also turns and continues his walk to where he has been standing. Holding out his hands he leans into the stone water catch.

The last time Overview had seen Tahvo they were disputing the identity of a fugitive from the U.S. Army. His picture was on a card that confirmed he had escaped a work crew unpinning landed spring loaded canister. He had escaped the bomb squad. He had refused the commands of the man holding a rifle and chased a truck, loaded with refugees down a mined road, then disappeared aboard the truck. The condition of the road, or fear of underground mines was very real. They could be connected underground into a single explosive device. Springing one could explode them all. That possibility dampened the idea of pursuit. The escapee was eluding the difficult situation of bomb squad life-expectancy. The mortality table exposed to danger everyone in the mine field. The bomb squad froze in position. Unexploded fragmentation bombs were never something to trifle with. Most bomb squad members were prisoners. They were typecast. A catastrophe often created very little dialogue other than the unraveling of the drama. Every explosion was an occupational hazard. Their lives embraced inherent danger.

Both Tahvo and Overview knew the escapee. They hadn't seen him since the return of Military Police who saw the situation as placing several witnesses between a rock and a hard place. Both Tahvo and Overview were witnesses to his escape, but neither felt any repercussions from not chasing him down and taking him into custody at the time of his flight. No one wanted to chase the bomb squad refugee down the explosive and soft earth road. They would eventually feel constriction and pressure from the Military Police. But at the point of escape they hadn't shot the fleeing man. Overview had refused to shoot a fellow United States military man according to his statements. They hadn't aided in his escape but hadn't prevented it.

As Overview went around the fountain trying to close in on his yokefellow in the escape they had witnessed, he assumed correctly that Tahvo had turned the water works on to start the fountain. Overview wanted a closer view. Tahvo was proud of himself. Watching the reaction of the man he knew to be ordinarily civilized and rational acting made him very nervous. Overview knew this performance by the water fountain jet spray would attract a crowd. He worried that someone, or something, might come out of abandoned buildings behind Tahvo. His thoughts stopped when he thought what might happen when the powerful attraction of spraying water brought a crowd to the broken town. Overview watched as Tahvo reached down into the pool and cupped a hand of water then brought it to his nose sniffing it. He wasn't trying to waylay Tahvo. But the water should be turned off. For now the geyser should be shut down.

The two men were very different. Where Tahvo saw immediate use for the water, Overview merely thought of a frantic crowd reaction this could bring. Tahvo shouted across the water in a voice that caught Overview off guard. "It breathes and this is life," he said. Overview wanted to open up a conversation, and said the first friendly thing that came into his head. "You can have as much water as you want, but you can't put a claim on this waterspout."

Tahvo recognized the rational intelligence in the remark, and glanced for a moment at the reflection of Overview in the pool of water between them. Overview was a devoted public servant. Tahvo was devoted to his own food and water needs. This could lead to liberation from an impoverished background. Tahvo could use the fountain as a business. Tahvo was devoted to chasing money and its freedom. Ahead of him he saw plenty of light. This fountain was a part of civic machinery Tahvo could operate.

Tahvo looked over at Overview and choosing to joke said, "This would make a nice piece of property."

Overview responded with a question. "If you can turn this on, can you turn it off?"

Tahvo considered the question. The question made him feel for a moment that his shoes were stuck to the stone beneath him. His response would have been a simple, "Yes." He stopped when Overview noticed a shadow moving on the fourth floor of a broken building behind Tahvo. The expression on Overview's face gave pause to Tahvo. He did not turn to look, and interpreted the expression for what it was. He thought how completely exposed he was in the middle of a battleground. His prowess for battle was limited to personal self-defense. The magnetism of the place here was awesome and awful.

Overview crossed the ground to his Jeep now with a hand on his sidearm. He shouted back to Tahvo, "If you can turn it off, I'll give you a ride to the rail station."

The whistle of the approaching railroad engine could be heard some distance away. At the moment Tahvo was in charge of the spraying, potable water. It was a great improvement over the pivoted pole with the bucket and counterweight that preceded it. Tahvo had the incredible talent of the fountain in the tips of his fingers. He thought the offer for a ride to the train reliable so shouted, "Just a second."

Tahvo explained to Overview how the underground chamber beneath the water fountain was made after he climbed underneath it, and torqued it off. Overview got into his Jeep and backed slowly away from the center of the plaza until he had felt his rear wheels lower onto the dirt beside the manmade pavement. This was no time for a siesta. His eyes focused on the vacant and destroyed buildings around the plaza. No one appeared. Overview was surprised how quickly Tahvo reemerged from the manhole, scooted it over, and jogged toward the Jeep. When Overview asked about the underground works Tahvo answered proudly.

"The main line splits into a T, left and right, and the main continues at the junction for about twenty feet where there is another valve. That turns the fountain on directly. Both the left and right T run about three hundred yards but are capped at the end and are underground. There is supposed to be fire hydrants, or other fountains, but they never got built. There is a door that locks under the fountain, but the key doesn't work so I use this." He held up a small metal bar about six inches long that he'd used to pry the door.

When Overview and Tahvo were in the Jeep and on the way to the rail station, he wondered if he and Tahvo could have a productive relationship. Overview looked over at Tahvo and realized that despite the bleak surroundings and the war zone, Tahvo was very healthy. This gave Overview an optimistic feeling. He was optimistic he could derive a coordinated relationship in terms of communication and feedback. Overview always relayed information back to the highest levels. Overview was considered a field man, expert in both weapons and psychology. This in spite of the fact that he didn't have a college degree in either field. He did not flash credentials. Overview wasn't known for quick answers, or retort. He was more known for laughing about witty answers that occurred to him only when it was too late.

Without question he was building a strong relationship. Overview took the road less traveled when he backed the Jeep away from the plaza. Following side streets and little used roads they were stunned by the eerie look of destroyed streets, and dwellings. It gave him a monstrous feeling as they drove along the road. He was not able to hide this from Tahvo. All the property along the road was owned by villagers gone from the scene of the battle. What lay next in store for this ghost town? Tahvo kept his eyes on the road as they drove slowly. The slow, motorized crawl through each deserted section of town was procession-like.

Tahvo spoke in a gloomy tone. "Like an imaginary place isn't it. Like it's not real. Who could make this much devastation? This was mayhem."

Overview looked over at him and said, "It is a nightmare for sure. But it is very real. Who could make this up? What do you mean?"

Tahvo said, "When you write a book you make the place up where the book takes place.

Overview turned and looked at him.

Tahvo continued. "I read something. Animal Farm. That's an imaginary place. Dracula. That's an imaginary place. Treasure Island. An imaginary island." Tahvo shifted in his seat and looked over at Overview, adding to his comment. "Mummies too. When you read a story about mummies they make the place up. Someplace in Egypt."

Overview smiled over at him and said, "Egypt is a real place," and Tahvo answered, "Yes, but mummies don't walk around the place."

Overview laughed at this and nodded his head. Overview stopped. The road was blocked by a calf.

The calf in the road was not in Overview's way. When he stopped

Tahvo didn't get out. Overview stepped lightly from the Jeep after it coasted to a halt twenty feet from the animal. "Must have keep it indoors. Where else could you put it?" The calf showed no alarm at Overview approaching. He held out his hand holding a strap he'd pulled from the back seat. The calf bolted and moved ten feet from the center of the road. Overview's swift movements, steady and fast, put him right in front of the calf and he slipped a loop over the calf's neck. Then the calf bolted again. Overview pulled it close and fell on top of it. This was a cowboy move he didn't want to make. He wondered if he could still wrangle the tiny beast.

On top of the noisy calf he looked back at Tahvo and yelled, "Get over here, and bring something to tie him."

Tahvo stood in the Jeep in his seat, and laughed. He said, "Use your belt," but Overview had no intention of using his own wardrobe and yelled, "Come on."

Tahvo got up and jumped out of the Jeep. He pulled another six-foot strap from the seat and walked over to Overview who was trying to calm the calf. With one free hand he pulled a serrated knife from an arm sheath and held it up.

To Tahvo he said, "Cut that in half. Tie his back legs."

Tahvo did as he was told, wary of the knife. Overview stood on his feet. With its back legs tied the calf stood up and bounced away, then fell over.

Overview said to Tahvo, "Tie them front legs."

Tahvo said, "I'm not a steer wrestler," but did as he was told, kneeling on the calf's neck and tying a quick knot around the front legs.

Then the calf stopped making noise and lay silent. Overview put the knife back in its sheath, stepped over to the calf, and picked the tiny animal up. Less than a month old he held him in his arms as he walked over to the Jeep and placed the calf in the back seat. Tahvo stood motionless through all this. Tahvo wondered if he would get the same treatment later. So he hung back from the Jeep as Overview made sure the calf was tied down and could not leap from the Jeep once it started moving. Overview could tell Tahvo was considering leaving him at this spot so he stood with his hand on the steering wheel, and looked over at Tahvo who was standing in the road with his arms hanging loosely at his side. Overview knew the burdensome task to corral the tiny calf had raised an alarm in him. It was typical that it would sound alarm signals in the local native's head.

Then Tahvo raised his hand and asked a question. "What's that calf worth to you?" he said.

"What?" said Overview.

"What's that calf worth to you? I'll give you ten dollars for it."

Overview smiled and looked at the beast in the back seat. "How about twenty," he said.

Tahvo smiled after a pause, and said, "Fifteen."

Overview looked again over at Tahvo and wondered how much money Tahvo had. Twenty dollars wasn't much. But that was a lot of money for this bombed out neighborhood. The calf was a valuable prize. "What do you have in mind for him?" Overview asked.

Tahvo just smiled. "I thought I could do business down at the train."

Overview replied, "Well, that's where I'm going so let's see what kind of business we can get over there."

Tahvo thought again at the idea of himself rounded up by Overview in the Jeep. This might mean a work shift at the train which was now whistling within hearing of the two men. Both men's smarts focused on the coming attraction a train offered. Tahvo got in the Jeep. Age demands balance. Every age needs encouragement by a balanced adult. Encouragement sometimes comes from crowd-sourced ideas.

By the train the girl and luggage

Pipe one's eye, more slang, more weeping

CHAPTER FOUR

The arrival of the train to Stevo Brakeman's station brought former villagers and part of the dis-banded army to the station so they could retake their village homes. Large by number, and varied by sex and age they waited on the outskirts of town along the railroad track. They wouldn't stop the train, but they were very near the tracks.

At the station walkway a force of thirty security agents have been hired to secure the train. They had arrived by plane at an airfield nearby. These re-enforcements included a new intelligence gathering compound crew, a nine person assemblage, and a railroad station house crew. Most had military grade weapons training.

The train was not a long one. It would loop here and turn around. People accompanying the train included local and international dignitaries. This is a peace train. The goal is a resettlement of the village. Most trains don't come to an end in the frontier area. This was specifically made to be a delivery vehicle for the village where a gifted populous had made plastic containers, twenty-four hours a day until the outbreak of hostilities brought the village to an end. Employment in the village had been a sought after job. Making plastic forms made the village an industrial center. Afterwards came service centers to the community for food and clothing, and everyday items. There was also a guano processing plant nearby which packaged fertilizer. Seen as a nuisance it was located on the village's outskirts. That marshy grassland area sometimes produced a methane gas. When the gas ignited a light over the watery area it was called a jack-o-lantern. There were flocks of birds swimming in the deeper pools of water. They nested in the grass leaving collections of guano. Dried and put into bags, the commodity of guano brought a surprising price.

Both the factory centers had some air conditioning built into the plants. When the hostile army came they took over the plants. The village's new plaza and the factories had both been decimated by long-range guns, and then raiders who sent crews and weapons by train. They had such an overwhelming force, that the battle was over quickly, but not before destruction of the village's premier attractions. What the village held out to people from the community before the battle, a factory job and a public plaza for trade, were all destroyed.

The village population had for the most part avoided the fighting. No significant force was raised by the village when the invading army took over. Most of the population fled. The population could not flee up the railroad line because hostilities were ongoing in that area. In the direction away from the railroad was a mixture of swamp and bird feed area, dry desert land, and a distant mountaintop some five miles away. A blinking red light near the top of the mountain marked the location of an old English gold mine. The mine had changed hands over the decades many times. New drilling and excavation techniques brought new investors, and the visibility of the mountainside site brought ambitious paramilitary units, and tribesmen. The Englishman in possession of the titles of ownership had minimal success with deep tunneling. That had halted with the battlefield developing below. The battle scene was visible by telescope. The Englishman's plant and mine location were still occupied and well-guarded. There were however, unknown numbers of tribesman gathering in the area, maybe in a warring reclamation effort. Or, a possible strike against a convoy. Persons inside the mining facility had taken the opportunity to get to the train or board themselves up. Everyone who knew about it, and the armies on the battlefield below, wanted a peek inside the mine. It was now the most visible resource to people standing below the blinking antenna, many with nothing but hopes.

Overview had been at the communications compound site for nineteen weeks. He sought cover there once, but more often stayed at the mine. Not underground, but in the antenna shack. When he realized they were going to be receiving a train, and it would be outbound within twenty-four hours, he packed a light duffel, armored his vehicle, shifted ammunition to underground, and left ammo drops at the mountain, and ammo at a cliffsite where goods were traded by chiefs. He secured the remainder inside the train station and traded for a large, oversize, plastic and rubber, water tank the size of a freight car. A Russian military made, giant, hard rubber tank. It could be filled with concrete. It was Army Engineer size, sturdy enough to support light wheeled traffic. Empty it could be floated. Filled it could be sunken as a support wedge. It could be part of a structure. Another trade was for a hollow balloon. These were used to make inflatable tanks and stored all around Britain before the invasion of France. Now used as construction supports for land/water personnel bridges. Or, a swimming pool.

Tahvo sat in the front seat of the Jeep with his arms around the calf. Overview was considering planting Tahvo at the water fountain with the dirigible, or whatever the containers were but he wanted one of the town's secrets from Tahvo. About the gold mine. The cursed gold mine. The cursed gold mine that many claimed had already cracked the mountain's base. Fifteen excavation chambers below the first chamber they had discovered and cleared out the mine's most valuable, and highly guarded "vug." There were bankets of gold bearing fragmentary rock. That was thirty-seven years, ago. Some believed there might be another golden age for the mine. Now the yield was nil. But that one fortune had been immense. Now the English Lord bought mostly river traces of gold. These he displayed in the front of his office at the claim. He had only landed here once by helicopter. His agents and mine supervisors came from Thailand.

Any saboteur would take the mine to be a resource, or a staging ground. They had dynamite and vehicles the size of earth movers. Around the grounds, cameras consistently recorded personnel movements on the property. Putting the earth mover on the road would not be as difficult as one might think. If you were reckless enough. Fuel could be driven in a truck and the truck could follow down the mountain. That would require a partner in cahoots.

The showroom of the mine was filled with cases displaying maps, blueprints and quartz placer findings. There was a case for processed bars of gold ingot emblazoned with plate marks, and a case for purchased specimens. The manager/operator, a Thailand engineer and his brother, a male nurse and local doctor, discovered and sold copper on the property. That held promise. They had traded for consumer goods with a Chinese trader aboard the arriving train. He was bringing dry goods, including rice and bulk foodstuffs, plus some frozen and green grocer vegetables. All ready for consumption. The Chinese trader aboard the train name was named Estaban Dae. He was here to see about the Chinese miners, and other friends at the mine. He had been raised in China. His real national birthright was Peru on the west coast of South America. Returning there after an average adulthood, he was now multicultural, and multilingual. He was like Stavros and was arriving on the train. He was also an agent of the train. Business here then he was bound for Egypt.

Estaban Dae was here to buck the line. The overrunning of the town by its own townspeople meant a large part of the former citizenry would board the train at the station upon the train's departure. Estaban was here to take Genius the lion with him. Touma Thomaz had sold the lion to a zoo. In a city made near enough by the train. This large type of transaction would clear the compound of Genius for the incoming communications crew. No one likes being confronted by the lion, the king of beasts. They reek of nature. A zoo would be best for the domesticated lion. Better than a rugged mountainside home. Estaban Dae was just picking the lion up, and traveling by train on a distant trip. On his own flat car. The cage aboard was too small for the length of the train trip for the big male lion. He would have to find a larger one.

The train traveler's railroad journal. Updated.

The train's arrival will be marked by a turning point. Sunday it left for its destination. I still feel good. Fresh food of the mind is with me. If I steal from a "thought for the day" booklet do I have to repay it? Shall I honor my debt? A friend on the train is so excited she offers to pay to see my luminous dial electric Swiss Army watch. It is dark, and I must hold it up to my eye to read it. For breakfast this morning I ate the whole bowl of jam with toast. We see supply dumps every ten miles or so, by the railroad track. All along the track, people are building plastic coned bins. They at first will live in them. We stop next to a station where an animal stampede has removed fences and grass. At the station stop they sold us cooked meat. Some kind of cooked meat.

We can see an oil field from the train. It is below and a plane flies alongside us. We stay on the train at the next stop. The aggravating remarks I want to make about other people on the train I don't regret. I am sleeping in a reclining chair. There is no news other than news on the progress of the train. I am glad the train trip continues. Everyone is standing and looking out the windows. I feel as if the trip is more than an adventure. Passengers are holding their baggage. I want the trip to be over. I am grinning at the possibility that our trip is over. I am an experienced traveler. My next stop, one that is familiar, is a possible new start. I am elated and humbled. I am grateful my family has been on my mind throughout this trip. I planted a garden in spring the last time through. I will see what springs from God's eternal earth when I see it again.

Touma Thomaz has been working all along at paperwork destruction which means shredding files. He began with large regional maps. Keywords and regions connected to the expanded database were part of his find. This was for academics. Incidents had been mapped to the region, and pictures of locals taken by locals. He was shredding all the maps no matter how small the scale. Local residents were remembered by Touma as he shredded pictures of them.

Estaban Dae was returning to the area known as Departure Road Station. Others called it the Railhead. The departed armies had not left behind a marble palace, or luxurious green gardens. The army hadn't come to attract, and then command a prince. A crystal clear lake with a green pasture might be in a future landholder's dream. But today the army that forted itself in the stone and marble square was gone. The army was dismantled. Everything else, meaning the fountain and the radio tower were left intact. Princes among the natives and rebels from great distances had fought here under the sky marked by the Departure Road Station mine. Estaban Dae was taking on a role similar to the communications unit. Upon arrival he was earmarked for shipping out. Estaban Dae would also like to pack up his architectural find, and priceless discovery. A golden sleeve that natives further up the rail track had pressed onto a wooden carving, the size of a wash bucket. The gilded pipkin had been flattened by a motorized vehicle. This treasure looked like an old face, shiny and golden. It scared the living daylights out of anyone staring into its rolled gold grimace. He was hoping it could be dated pre-Shaka Zulu. If not, the cast of thick gold and silver could be made into coin. Private mint coins commemorating South Africa. Temples of this region were meant to portray the daily life of the gods. Not all gods lived in palaces. Some lived among the tribes. This piece of golden treasure could find its way to a museum or a dealer. Estaban Dae would help in this course of action, but only for a profit.

Captain Overview with one more covert mission to complete was ready to ship stateside.

Overview's last covert action was being called by him a training exercise. Captain Overview had one more covert mission to complete, and he was ready to ship back home. The bullion fringe on Overview's dress uniform was a noble golden metal. He was bringing the military unit into something he would later term a family matter. Or, a dangerous situation and a possible tragedy in the making.

In order to start with a common language he was going to employ a manual entitled "How to Prepare and Conduct Military Training." This was so that the counterpart team, the other guys, would have to share a language with his team. This would bring safety he hoped. It would allow him to create orders that might catch a naïve opponent. It was a cat-and-mouse game. He wanted to find out a hostile resistance place of manufacture for legal drugs including antibiotics, and pain relievers offered by an efficient pharmacy, shipping to customers throughout the world. Someone's aunt got crazy, disjointed mad, his sister, because of a shipment calling for adult guidance. Oxy-except. Oxy-shout. An opioid pain reliever. Effective and addictive. Drug companies knew. Most doctors also now know. Now it was being shipped to Overview's niece. Similar initials in their names led phone salesmen to call her. He was stepping into the way of that, and closing down those contacts. First he had to know who they were. So a meeting was being planned by him. Under military supervision. This meant Overview would get a chance to talk to the pharmaceutical drug dealers, after finding out their identities. He had a place on a map where approximate contours were not up-to-date, and the Captain felt he could catch their team out of position. Overview wanted the distance between himself and his quarry to be ten yards, not ten thousand. Aside from that field officer dispatch there were other records and documents bring critiqued.

The focus of a detailed report circulating was twofold. Extenuating circumstances interrupted its course. First, an Army typist currently ranked in the top one percent for speed in the entire Armed Forces was the subject of this blue book. The Army limits its typists to fifteen tests in the center for communications testing facility. One Army typist displayed excellent workmanship at over one hundred thirty-five plus words per minute when she used AI, artificial intelligence for script. Proper key strokes for phrase selection made her very competent in the first document.

The typist was, however, a dangerous, and combative suspect. An Army typist and first lieutenant of the Communications section where she was stationed, she was sitting in one of the compound trailers. She had been keeping the bad guys out of business for the Army for quite some time. She had driven a motorcycle through the countryside. With her status and ability in the Armed Forces she was here to take care of a special problem. The best typist in the Army. The top one percent.

The second part of the report, a white paper, described the Cold War between the U.S.S.R., and the United States. Her commander was in some ways involved in the Cold War. A relationship between the U.S. and the U.S.S.R. was first begun in nineteen-thirty-three. In that year the original *King Kong* film was a colossus movie success. The animation techniques set new standards. In 1933 the United States was the giant figure hello-ing the Bolsheviks led by Lenin. In 1933 the Soviets were officially recognized by the United States. In 1946 Britain's Alan Nunn was jailed for giving atomic secrets to the U.S.S.R. Russia sponsored rigged elections in Poland in 1947. In 1958 the Soviets launched a dog into space. A cosmic space race commenced with the U.S.S.R. and the United States expediting men and resources to be the first to the moon. Booster rockets and space modules were built. Astronauts and cosmonauts vied to be the first. Gantry towers were built on concrete launching pads. Innovation developed. Pioneers from both countries began a race to put the first man in space. The Soviets got the first man in space in 1961. In the year 1983, President Ronald Reagan was still describing the U.S.S.R. as an evil empire.

The communications post Brigadier General, Stevy Thomasine, was part of the U.S.A. and U.S.S.R. détente. He wrote papers in his field that studied an eight-man emergency committee that ousted Gorbachev. Later they returned him to power when the coup was opposed by Boris Yeltsin.

During the Cold War, both the U.S. and the Soviets focused on the study of the properties of concrete. Multistage booster rockets sent off from an aggregate concrete base. In the Soviet Union the study of concrete was a scientist's occupation. In the United States concrete is big business, and specialized. Science that reveals new structural modifications for rocket bases is a possible football. Money for information is possible. The U.S.S.R. freed the nations of Latvia, Lithuania and Estonia. Independent and free and independent. That was good business. Good business was also a study where competitive couriers exchange cash for the study of concrete stability. The Soviet State Council insists it abolished the KGB. No other agency has been created for the purpose, of international concrete fact finding.

The Brigadier General Stevy Thomasine was going to be part of an airdrop that would take place off the coast. A spy would cooperate with complete fullness if the Air Corp of the Army would drop him from an aircraft in one of the few countries that do not allow extradition to the United States. His role was played as a maintenance supervisor. He copied records in the facility they were using for concrete studies. General Thomasine was going to be present when the double agent would parachute into what he hoped would be a new life. For him this was a new step in his career.

The compound commander, a Brigadier General was a workaday officer. He kept his head down in the foxhole, and employed strategies with available field resources. He brought in aircraft and artillery fire. He was someone superior officers requested take care of special problems. His highest ranked assistant was one of the best typists in the Army. The commander's service record read like a letter of achievement. He was assigned the highest level of training and scholarship. The reason for this was his view of ethics. He saw morality as a universal value. His approach to approved standards was something he was willing to discuss. He was in the Army, and interested in social change. Little of that was available. His job as a battle tactician was adaptive. He developed resources and based decisions on research, deploying what was available. His greatest achievement was a take home essay that won him a general's star. How do you count the words?

His assistant commander Steffie Thom was at the moment following up on an affidavit of forged endorsement. The Lost/Stolen Check affidavit required a signature under the penalty of perjury attesting, "I did not receive any benefit, or value from the proceeds of the check listed above." All this good reportage in spite of the fact that she had just committed the atrocious act of throwing a drinking glass into the shower while it was occupied by a bather. She did this intentionally. She was not retaliating for the $1194.14 cash disbursed by a misplaced check. She shattered the glass because of what she thought of the ceiling above her created by the man in the shower. Then she escaped to her trailer. The man in the shower went ballistic. He demanded an end to the communications blackout. Steffie's behavior was going onto a report from an officer just granted leave.

The granting of leave at this time was an ordinary matter. To appear for a leave request at the time of evacuation in Lieutenant Thom's office/trailer meant shoving aside clutter, and relaxing through an interesting process of transfer. Steffie was sincere, expert, and straightforward. She was also reliable. The tossing of the drinking glass had been an act of frustration. That the glass was broken in the shower did not require a sexual harassment inquiry. Emotional distress was present, but offensive verbal conduct was not. To be honest she had taken this first step to prevent "constructive discharge." She actually worried that someone might think what she had done was clever.

The bather in the shower was Large Type, Touma Thomaz, Security and Information, U.S. Army Lieutenant, 2nd. The vandal he protected, Steffie Thom. This avoided the applied mores and principles of other commissioned officers. A slight tremor in the ground might have been an earthquake he claimed, or it might have been an artillery round. Echoes are tough to distinguish. With Steffie Thom he was applying for a field upgrade, and de-enlistment. The process was necessary, both personally and professionally. He was going back to States. Back to the FBI. Back to one of the wonders of the world's greatest cities, Las Vegas, Nevada. For the FBI that might mean a canine patrol.

Canine patrols roam through newer skyscraper casinos. Or, event centers, or through the back drive of the casino most frequented by Presidents of the United States. Every living President has visited the casino across from the empty lot that is next to the current President's Tower. The standalone condominium tower is marked with a high visibility ownership sign. The building is a classic challenge to other towers, and owners. Every living President has been on the grounds across the street. That includes visits, and gatherings directed by their wives. At the opening of the tower across from the condominium tower, the builder and his wife welcomed George Bush Sr., and his son at the casino's opening. The then sitting President George W. Bush was invited to the initial kick-off week. Also at the highly publicized and well-attended grand opening were several feather-boa-trailing, green-eyed, female flappers. Whomever was the most glamourous would require debate conducted in moot court. The most faithful companion, man's best friend hobnobbed along the corridors. The owner said, "This is your playground. Be smart. We have gathered you intentionally. We have gathered the best minds here today. Have fun." This poses a Secret Service security issue. An FBI dog can be man's best friend. His boon companion on an obvious journey. These roamed throughout the grand opening.

That is where Touma was intending to return. To Las Vegas and his life. He had completed five years of commitment after his initial enlistment. Now he wanted benefits, including an FBI job recognizing his field accomplishments since training under cover. Out of the country it had not been an issue. He was enlisted under an assumed name. Now it would be an accomplishment to overcome that level of anonymity. Disappearing for five years is not easy. Exception for this disappearance would have to be acknowledged, and regarded as temporary relocation. He need someone to recommend his advancement strongly, and with passion. He wanted more furor than a pastor's letter. He wanted a more fiery recommendation.

Touma's desire to enter Armed Forces enlistment had been hastened by his FBI job. His work had been undercover as a concierge with a prominent downtown hotel. He wore a name tag and realized he could not continue using a false name in his own home town. He joined the Army with a pre-enlistment agreement that included clandestine service. At first that meant just reading messages across international cables. Now it was news gathering in a foreign country. Watching satellites. Recognizing hostile forces and keeping track of their movements. He employed a United Nations approach widely followed by intervening forces.

Touma was an Italian. His classic idea of romance was to introduce himself to every girl he thought spontaneous enough to be interested in him. He tendered offers graciously. Being nose-to-nose, and cheek-to-cheek were the kind of test scores he was after. Any dark-haired woman, or possibly a tall, handsome redhead, or a tiny blond in a sundress would fall for his rendition of "Embrace for Me, Around, Around." His active love life was "off the hook." Lately, he and Steffie Thom had been trying to set the phone back into its cradle. Their arguments focused on the claim that he had learned about love the hard way. The other subject was usually "What is the most important thing to save money for?"

Touma was up-to-date with the posted and diminishing man-hours budget. Personnel were leaving the compound. Everyone was well along in a well-planned move from the reserve within the shadow of the mountain, near the edge of the desert. Bedouin, the desert natives, were returning from the most remote areas. Touma's idea of love had changed to a Bedouin bride. To believe she was a Bedouin, bound for the U.S.A., and Las Vegas seemed unlikely. But likely it might be. She had joined a caravan making its way through the desert. Her goal was no mirage. The caravan had been resting at a fertile oasis. Her trousseau was being prepared for nuptials.

Something about Touma's past life as an undercover FBI agent disturbed him. The irony of his past disturbed him more than insensitive foreign troops bringing weapons to this war zone. Undercover as a casino concierge he had seen pointless his exposure to life's petty offenses including fake ID, and age requirements. He was turned off by these offenses. He had portrayed a much younger naïve kid. He had worn a red-striped shirt with black suspenders, and exchanged sideways looks with colorful, well-dressed women. He chose instead to reach levels of advancement by taking chances. The Armed Forces had been that place.

He wanted something more than outrage, then placement of a john law dragnet over his fellow man's unrighteous conduct. What he felt about himself turned out to be true. He had been an animated, robotic character. His behavior was based on the worst aspects of others. He felt an honest living showing his own face was still in him.

Touma felt Steffie Thom should take his suggestion. Touma recognized Steffie had an indefinable quality. She and he both knew in this area something was about to change with them both.

All around the country villagers were returning, and the United Nations peace keeping force was present. The end of armed conflict meant relocation. Where are you shipping out to? Everyone's exit from the communications facility was meant to be a simultaneous maneuver without surprise. This required a military level of execution. There is a high standard for this kind of training. It is principally language oriented, with an objective in the forefront. Military maneuvers are not often self-paced. A common language helps guide everyone toward a successful field exercise. Readiness is judged by status of personnel. Morale is important in this process. Towards that end, an obvious improvement in morale, at the camp and the campground was encouraged with the personnel divided into halves. Both had very good outlooks.

lady elephant walk

More orange squash, means more money.

CHAPTER FIVE

Stephanie was wasting nothing learning about elephants. Would Sam help her get a last minute performance out of the lion? This might be key, and was scheduled to happen at the train. The lion was in send-off mode. Sold to a zoo. The transportation cage was scheduled for arrival at the train station. Steffie was counting on Sam to help her get smooth performance out of Genius. He was not a foolproof lion, performance wise. Steffie hoped that an elephant would aid in the spectacular exhibition feature of having and maintaining a caged lion. This was going to be a display meant to impress. A spectacular extravaganza by the railhead impresario, Steffie Thom.

You might think elephants are prettier than lions. Or, maybe you don't care. Someone who does care might realize elephants have much greater cognitive powers when compared to a lion. They really are much smarter. They can be extremely tame. A daily bath is nearly mandatory for a working elephant. The closest an elephant wants to come to a lion is if the herd shelters the young, and the male bull elephant can get his trunk around the shoulders of the lion. Then, give it a squeeze. A mis-placed foot could crush any part of the feline cat. The herd will shelter young calves from a large cat. Even when they are talent show elephants, or movie star elephants, they are extremely protective of their young, and human animal trainers. If you are going to tie an elephant to a tree you must get his ears stuck between two trees. African and Indian elephants have few differences, but one is distinct. The Asiatic elephant's trunk ends in one finger. The African elephant's trunk ends in two fingers.

Elephants are usually stealthy when on the move, or around people who are watching the show, or backstage with show people making the performance come alive. The elephant will pause when he enters a doorway, bending down and walking at a careful pace on his knees. After he is through the door, the elephant rises then will allow strange riders to climb aboard. On the way to the paddock he taps his trainer on the shoulder and leaves him at his trailer. After the show is over it can reach out with a trunk to compensate for his next shuffle. An elephant can be sly, slow, and shifty.

Steffie thought the elephant would be an awesome sight beside the train, and therefore the most powerful colossus present. Bigger than a tank. Bigger than a personnel carrier. The biggest thing on the station platform. This was not just a movie stunt. The returning villagers would react positively to the sight of the well-trained, but wild, part of the jungle. It would be a good stunt. The local water retrieval system had been the elephant, and one long, flexible rope down the community well. A new and modern water system had replaced the elephant.

The elephant's rider was well-off riding, and convinced that the elephant might retire an affiliated actor. At this stage his performances would not eclipse the best movie stunt ever. Pulling the jungle and all the skeleton midgets into an opening the size of a large paper cup, at the end of a movie about an ancient mummy. Mummies and skeletons. The movie arcs surreal, designing a supernatural, giant, black scorpion walking upright. The elephant would have to go some to outdo that movie bit. Still, the animal's handler insisted the elephant was an artist. Huzzah! What a great day it is!

"Sitting, then arrange my station." Steffie was "speaking," again. She was handing over transfer preparations to an assistant. The assistant was going to join her in the United States Infantry School for Airborne Troops. She had completed her own transfer papers.

Airborne training for parachute regimental infantry. A parachute training course can open self-confidence and aggressive spirit. The entire process is part of high activity, leadership level, mental and physical training. Generally it is for elite fighting men and women.

To begin with the process required formidable rite of passage. Fifteen copies of your orders were issued to you. You were expected to have a proper shave and haircut and begin the process at 1200 hours. A list of equipment, clothing and uniform include required items such as five pairs of cushioned soled socks. Eyeglasses of military issue were recommended. It was requested you apply a high shine on your boots and wear two sets of dog tags. Parachutist helmets were the *only* headcover allowed in the training area.

Steffie and her assistant, a physical training expert, Nevet, a dark-haired Asian of Filipino and Hawaiian descent, were planning to spend lunch break with twenty-five minutes of paperwork and materials from a guide for airborne students. The military guide had a lift flap, revealing required solutions. It wouldn't be easy getting through that. Opening another manual, she checked the work of Touma Thomas who had been unfolding solutions to requesting and adjusting mortar fire. Everyone was interested in the paperwork. There were required solutions and you were expected to offer specific detail. Everyone recognized the possible occupational hazard.

Steffie had a parachute jump story. Jumping from a two hundred fifty foot tower she'd suffered a calf injury. Yet she had performed a parachute landing fall score in the top one percent of training scores. The tower training week course was forty hours. This included jumps plus classes taken over five days. Training came from parachute tower drops from two-hundred-fifty-feet towers. Or, thirty-four-foot towers. These rehearsed falls lasted throughout tower training week. Jump week was off-base and a specialty position and indicated a high level of training. A big vacation week. Air travel aboard aircraft staffed by military personnel. Nearly anywhere. Pinpointing coordinated strongholds. Twice gear up and jump down. Steffie was working on her exit plan. Her jumps came at the top five percent of high altitudes. An injury to her calf required balance tests and re-certification. She would be within six weeks, re-certified. This was her conditioning at the highest point of her athletic life.

The General Stevy Thomasine's compound had remained undiscovered by enemy forces. Conceivably because it was near the national border. A local chieftain had been a farmer. Before the outbreak of war he lived on his land. It touched a desert. Palms and thorny brush lined the sandy approach. Lions hungry, not spent would come from this part of the desert as they wandered looking for food. The compound also bordered a very thick forest. An overhead escarpment in its deepest regions was good cover, and rendezvous for animals and jungle natives. That jungle was a hiding place for apes.

The compound had grown into an effective social center. This was based on a presumption of the military personnel being friendly. Friendship was spoken in many languages. "We are leaving. Hope to see you again, soon" was an oft heard remark.

Near the train tracks, as the train approached there had gathered the three hundred and seventy-five families, all having a domicile within one mile of the center of town and possibly a workplace, or a job within five miles. What remained of houses and business was the utmost concern. A very human consideration.

The three hundred seventy-five families wanted back into their village. They were returning like ants. Their homes had been plundered. Their behavior was enhanced by an instinctive drive to return. They were motivated. The tiny ant with no capacity for memory is a robot. Little beyond instinct. Ants display this when they line up towards a broken candy bar. Do you fear being ruled by an intelligent computer?

For the returning villagers the destruction was inconsistent. For some it was minor. For others complete. Homes and property including vehicles and livestock herds plundered. Goats, mules, cattle, and other beasts including horses were wantonly decimated. Inside the overpass just along the communications corridor you could either wait for the supply train, or send a high-speed message. Most of the persons in the three hundred seventy-five families wanted to return to looted areas and see if their homes were intact. An airstrip kept the center of the cloverleaf under surveillance. A remote control drone circled at high altitude. The plane was in constant communication with the army compound by automated surveillance camera. Villagers were orderly so far.

Aboard the peace keeping train was a UN representative from Spain and Norway. Norway had funded the train. Spain was often in the position of offering language services. In this case English or Spanish, to the Norwegians. The Batuu language, Swahili, or Zulu, had not penetrated much of the Norwegian tongue. The UN representative from Spain was the foremost celebrity and dignitary, aboard the train. The train was also a delivery of UN forces to stations within the village. Troop strength was two hundred fifty troops, a mortar unit, and another company in reserve.

This railroad train station at the farthest point of the line was the center of attention from two opposite directions. The place was a turnaround. Another track, some sixteen miles distant, was coming through forest and across desert land to connect the western loop. The Spanish ambassador was among the supporters, and an owner of the business that supplied labor to the track. He was the mayor of a moving town of Spanish workers, numbering about seventy-five men, all working for his real estate development company. Right now they were working on the railroad track.

Most important to the ambassador after the completion of the railroad, was the opportunity that would open up from a different direction. One railroad track into town brings in one billion dollars. The second railroad track completes a circle that allows twenty-five more trains with a billion dollars to come into your town. The town chooses how much of each billion stays in their town. A certain number of banks can generate business that arrives by train. A bank within the community can be a sugar beet fairy, complete with concessions and dispensaries.

Aboard the Spanish ambassador's train was the mortar unit and peace keeping troops. No one expected there to be any action. These men were all green troops. French, Italians, Portuguese, Icelandics, and Germans. The Germans drove all the vehicles. The troops shared some language and racial/ethnicity differences. But they spoke common languages of English and Spanish. All the ethnicity and racial difference in the troops or in the town's people, made the people put to the test their endeavors. They would vie with each other for superiority.

A part of the townspeople wanted opera music upon returning. The librettos sounded like civilization and peace. A loudspeaker could be heard for miles. Others would eventually just stand in front of TV cameras brought by international peace keeping organizations, not controlled by government media. Townspeople addressed military personnel respectfully and gratefully, acknowledging the return of civil obedience. If it works, keep trying.

Instead of worrying about her transfer paperwork, Steffie worked on getting a mix of orchestral instruments and musicians to the station at the train's arrival time. A large group of local stringed instruments could perform during the provisions and aid disbursement from the train. This meant musicians could make loud noise and stand behind their musical effetery. Plus, a musician will always defend the stage for his instrument. They did have the common language of music. No one was expected to act zany. First on musicians, now first responders.

Steffie was almost ready for her own departure. Quite a taut string. She was also working on the return of medical personnel, and dispensary technicians to the site. At the moment it seemed a better idea to try to import veterinarians and teaching personnel. Too many sellers of alternative medicines with undesirable alternatives were available with their unorthodox therapies.

Two compassionate music teachers were importing a church group to sing in the native churches and build homes. The students brought stringed instruments, and favored violins. They were light and portable. The effect of more than a dozen cellos, violins, guitars, and banjos, could be deafening. It would require a director. They were on the train. Traveling as representatives of their church. About one dozen musicians would sing at the station. Seven members of a family from the village were going to be at the station. They were all musical artists who had performed at functions of the plastics plant. The plastics plant had employed about three hundred. They made shell containers for medical products, pills, lotions, see through plastic, mostly molded plastic, and caps. They shipped these bottles empty to the pill manufacturer. The plastic machines made plastic bottles of all types and sizes by the hundreds. This they did to music in the factory. Compulsive, driving music from local artists.

Each of these seven, fine musical artists would meet the train. Each would be going on a journey on the train. One was going to a hotel to work the hat check. Another would become a lawyer, libelous his issue, two would maintain musician status and travel, two become TV announcers, the last a script girl. These seven would leave on the train. What remained of houses and business, was the utmost concern. The three hundred and seventy-five families, all had a domicile within one mile of the center of town, and possibly a workplace, or job within five miles.

The Spanish United Nations ambassador was bringing aid materials, including his personal investment of three railroad cars of exotic fabric from coastal resources. These were meant to be used during wedding ceremonies, and distributed during public events. Part of his rail shipment was army surplus. Russian army surplus. He was also a spy for the Russian concrete conglomerate, known as Linkin. Not a real spy per se. The ambassador was ready to bring concrete resources and building materials to the rail line. Linkin was the name the natives called the Soviet state concrete maker. That was now the code name for the ambassador. Lincoln.

The train was on a very high-level priority list. Drones were scanning the town looking for looters or army and rebel personnel. So far, all were gone. The church attracted children, who were lost, or orphaned. At this point messages coming from Communications Specialist Touma Thomasine broke into the category of sling shot code words. Code words that were picking up new meaning even as they were being used. They were code makers. All were involved in it. They were creating the coded language. That's where this message initiated, "Lincoln is on the train without a rival and a policy statement. He will participate in this contest. Lincoln has a battery of writers, a director, and a hat man. Always works from a script." Their way of looking at the Spanish ambassador, was to call him a spy.

To disguise people and person events, new words were making their way into the codes. I might say, "important events in the lifetime" but mean, "give the patron a diploma," as the schedule of events unfolds, and the ambassador addresses the music students. With a diploma he hands out secure feelings to the town's new inhabitants. Changes are common. A new coded atmosphere surrounds ambassador "Lincoln." "Lincoln gives an opal to the fortune teller" means the one to get a new wedding dress is the fortune teller. The secret of code success? Study the script.

Stavros was waiting patiently for his shipment of chocolate. He had a traveling salesman problem. The shortest path to pass through a given set of points, once and only once. He hoped his usual matchless shipment would result in a cash turnaround. He was also suffering from the Abraham Lincoln effect. That is the tendency for an image up close to be unrecognizable until it is farther away. It has been said before, "Do we really want him getting his juice from a cactus?"

Negotiation Arvo, a tug-of-war in negotiation, this afternoon

CHAPTER SIX

The arrival of the train was a long hoped for event. Without the train and the comfort about to be unloaded at the train station, prospects for the re-vitalization of the village would be a forlorn hope, and any new enterprise would be in a helpless position. Everyone was of one mind and adapting. The community was lining up to absorb premium goods.

Meanwhile the Brigadier General, Stevy Thomasine was going ballistic. Re-phrase, the general was reprimanding orally his subject, Steffie, during she and Nevet's parachute training discussion. The level of discussion was very basic to Army education. The question was, "Do I turn my colleague in?" Would you confront another Army officer, if you knew the officer was cheating? Should I notice it? The reason of course, Touma Thomaz.

Steffie's and Touma's team player approach to a romance on the rocks was to ward off moral counseling, and guidance. Professional obligations were paramount. The general took the opportunity to explain to his technically competent and solid performer, Steffie, that maintaining composure under pressure was eighty-eight-percent of the time a good tactic. Without composure under pressure an officer's initiative, and field leadership, might be confronted by obstacles. Areas that need improvement are either, 1) needs some improvement or, 2) needs much improvement. Scholarship requires a different approach for each. The General was in the position of fortune teller, and needed to employ his sixth sense. Could they still work together? Any basis for complaint was going to be have to be made meaningful immediately. The warm approach would be tolerated. The last order in his verbal command indicated everything would go across Captain Overview's desk. It would come to his attention. There would be no official departmental letter at this time.

For a final project the general assigned Steffie the job of assembling files of each of the seven compound personnel who would be receiving official orders of transfer. The expectation of most was immediate travel. Dismissal of current duties would be made official. Steffie would have to pull up a special request order with the Regimental Commander to forward special conduct files. A special conduct file was the disciplinary file. This occurred when a soldier received a letter of reprimand, or had to display moral courage and admit, then write a personal description of his own regrets. These reports were filed. The speeding tickets, the lateness occurrences and unforgiven allegations were held in these files. These files might contain corrective actions that were attached in a statement in the cadet's own hand. Confessions. The type of thing the accredited staff (if approved by counselors and bugged offenders) would like to take to the bonfire. An official order like that would improve credentials. Eliminating a piece of each file was an obligation of the commanding officer transferring a candidate for new assignment. An inquisitor would not stumble over a capricious act. You would get a second chance. The commander could take something out and place it in their own file with an undated letter of reprimand addressed to the offender. These occurrences of file containment occurred so the commander could assure that an officer, or enlisted man's transfer, would go into effect. Something bad in your file would not jinx you. For some this was an unexpected piece of good luck. For some a miracle. The directive was to accomplish a transfer for each man under the general's command. He could recommend counseling and seal in his own transcripts a single act of deficient judgement. That piece of information would not follow you forever. It would follow the general. The file memo would be continued to be held if bad decisions had a certain relevance to you and your future conduct. If you could keep it together this could help your career path. It meant a favored past and a future with higher goals.

Steffie went down the list of people she needed this amnesty information on. Sometimes it is better just to ask the person themselves. What in your file are you asking a relieved view of?

Steffie would personally would like to see the quashing of the letter she wrote to the Department of The Army when she took an unauthorized two-hundred-and-fifty-foot parachute drop on the private property of the Safe Parachute Company. She was in the presence of fire department personnel with local connections. This occurred at night in an unguarded facility. The saving grace was that it was not on the training grounds, but on the private property of the Safe Parachute Company, near an airfield, and a state trooper station. This led to a civil complaint when discovery of the illegal entry onto private property was made. The state troopers had seen it before. The state troopers even knew which gate made for the best escape on foot. Kids had changed the lock themselves, but Steffie was left standing at the foot of the tower, while the fireman had no recommendations. Other than she accept the responsibility. All this led to lawyer services. The owners had seen it before. Too often in fact. Usually Safe Parachute didn't press charges against civil service, or army personnel. That was their customary response. This part of her file Streffie wanted expunged. That's what was going to happen to everyone's file before transfer. A piece of documentation would go missing from your file. This was going to make a difference in her future. Despite it the Army was keeping her at work on her present duties.

Steffie thought Overview was a hellraiser. Sometimes he was hell-bent-for-leather. H, E double hockey stick. He limped occasionally. His awkward walk was sometimes halting. He was highly regarded for his ability to register excellent bivouac performance scores. He responded early to the commander's requests for maintenance. He got the journeyman's job for water, electric, food, safety, and comfort. He made things go smoothly. He was deployable. What was in his discipline file? If it was an incident should it go away without undertones? Should it receive an order arms, eyes left salute? Should it be accelerated? Most people like to see peculiarities in their file disappear, double time. At a certain point a clerk had been cleared to begin a data entry on his foul-up. Something written under mandatory orders would be dropped from his file as soon as the company commander instructed Steffie to do it. His file would be truncated. Possibly if the material was sensitive, General Thomasine would excise it himself. The secret required oversight orders and official checks on the status of his security clearance. The note said simply, secret. Overview was headed for weapons re-certification. The rifle range.

What Overview was beginning to suffer from lately was loss of faith in a future he no longer controlled but played a part in. He was having trouble with his faith. His loss of faith was caused by self-imposed retirement. What was he left to do? For someone like him there wasn't a foursome with whom he would be drinking or, a girlfriend he could impose on. He would retire from the Army with his benefits. His mistake that led to his extradition back to the United States, was a case where he, the defendant, was proven innocent of wire fraud. The real charge originated when a galley assistant used a satellite phone at the price of twelve dollars a minute. The notes in his file with its lower portion torn was the story about Overview, and the telephone charges. He traded a de-enlistment for four months future active duty. This was due to containment, sitting in the brig while on an Army fleet vessel. A credit card was used without authorization and a female merchant marine assistant, under observation for suspicious phone calls, carried on procurement while on duty as galley chief of an Army marine vessel. By credit card.

Someone tried to move a couple million dollars by card, over the phone. These notes were being excised. Overview was galley chief, when the incident occurred. He was not involved.

After rifle range re-certification, Captain Oliver Overview, would tutor a college campus summer course, sign in to a recruitment office, and retire with full benefits. In four months. What he wanted to do after years in the Army was go to college. A college campus with ten thousand students.

Steffie had seen many files on the day of transfer, as principal assistant to the commander. She was in daily operation of the communications information filter. From Cadet, all the way through Commander. Issues might be as simple as body weight. A body fat test for a cadet, or an officer, can lead to serious consequences. A cadet would be asked to review his efforts with maturity and judgement. Let it be understood about the expectations of the U.S. Army. Details must be quickly understood. Motivating others is important. A good commander can be selfless and stay off the cookie dough.

What the Army does foremost is offer congratulations upon success. Good job. Well done. You should be proud of your effort. On behalf of the entire staff, we wish you to have continued success in the future. A successful commissioned officer who could be recommended for active duty is very valuable. This is obviously an outcome desired by most officers and cadets. An officer in good standing with training in squad and platoon leadership is worthy of special projects. Any project, other than being absent for call. Almost any specialty, or defined, and curious behavior can be overcome. Any instance of off-beat behavior.

Steffie had a professionalism and performance evaluation that followed her. She was still unable to correct those notes. She claims she was not the giggler. Her academic training had included Hispanic culture, economic geology, cultural anthropology, structural geology, concepts in biology, and military writing and correspondence. Despite a high degree of military bearing and appearance (and in some cases in the presence of other military personnel) she initially displayed the nervous habit of giggling during high-level meetings. She corrected that as she gained confidence. That document in her file was attached to the privacy act statement. The document also said she was anxious to learn everything about being an officer. She was rated in the upper center of mass in the lieutenant's profile. It was noted she excelled when physically and mentally challenged. She accepted all of her assigned tasks cheerfully, and accomplished them promptly. She was instrumental in planning and coordination of a day trip. Her spirit and sense of humor made the twenty-five kilometer road march easy. It was recommended she become comfortable with her role as an officer, overcome age issues, and be an asset in any branch of the armed services.

Camels waiting to train

Presto

Presto music is a rhythm very fast.

CHAPTER SEVEN

The river flows past. You cannot step in the same river twice. The river or process, or process of communication, or life moves in its process. The river is process. You can see from a spot on the river, or on the bank. Viewing from the bank is the military officer who planned the course for the good of the river. The river will become constant change.

The train with its peace keeping soldier cargo, and the mortar unit, with reserves, was experienced and expected to be in full control upon the arrival of the cargo train. They would be ready to react to enemy contact if there was any. The largest group of possible combatants were the villagers, grouped together near the edge of the village, and near the railroad track. Whatever chain of events could make that possible were to be avoided. The UN forces aboard the train were prepared to assault and destroy any enemy, should any force expose itself in the area. With air cover, and artillery fire, the unit could halt an aggressive advance and secure a defensive position. The decisiveness of the unit's commander was shown by early delegation of tasks. This began as the train passed the storage cloverleaf, and the UN unit noticed the large group of village personnel gathered. At the sight of the train the body of villagers began to move toward the station from the distance of one and one half-miles. Personal arms, hunting rifles and defensive weaponry seemed to glint in the sunshine, as the large group of villagers heaved a collective sigh, and headed toward the station. Training and observation set the trainload of soldiers on alert. The UN commander's intention was to accomplish his mission, and secure the avenues of approach to the station, occupy key terrain, and provide each of the soldiers with cover and concealment. With air cover, the high altitude plane in observation, the UN was prepared to take a defensive position if necessary. The primary objective was to let no opposing force move into the territory around the train station. Whether the villagers represented the possibility of a hasty or deliberate ambush, the soldiers were under orders and began preparations. The force aboard the train was prepared for a surprise, and contact positions and battle positions were identified. Verbal commands kept soldiers abreast of where every soldier stood on his mission, and readiness. Delegation of tasks was foremost, and early, so the purpose of an ambush and harassment would be avoided. The train passed the last check point, and a groan emanated from the villagers at the pace of the train. Its surprise appearance was causing a headlong rush in their midst. This activity caused re-organization of the armed military personnel already at the rail station. They knew what to do and with good control deployed themselves to possible attack positions. Boundaries were fluid. Most were temporary. The objectives of the units were later remarked upon in reports.

The length of the heavily guarded train was not long. It had separated a dozen miles back. It left behind a little over half of the train with a backup locomotive at a siding. Those cars were going to finish the trip when they got an "all clear." That was the reality discovered by the train station's commanding auditor. This was just part of the process. It was being created by civilian, not military personnel. Uncertainty surrounding the train's success on their mission, left it for all the forces of military and the citizenry to act with optimal efficiency. It was the opportunity of the train, including the railroad employees, the private citizens and businessmen riding with products on the train, to be the message of relief. Was there a message in the bounty of the train? The message made by the train was a spirit of optimism. The train was giving the villagers one chance to hear the message, in its correct context. The intelligent and useful relationship the train would establish, would be borne out in shared values. The time to step into the river was here. You cannot step in the same river twice. Many of the men aboard the train were officers with an overriding mission to deter war. Getting the job done would help insure a trip home.

On the train itself most of the soldiers from one of six countries had initially dedicated themselves to duties as engineers. That was the foremost training found in UN personnel. The mission of building roads and bridges is altered when they are pressed into service as aid givers to war's disaster victims. Based on a family commitment most men join the Army, and seek to become officers. Fathers support Army enlistment. An enlisted man seeks a commission as an officer. He has noticed the differences between being an enlisted man, and being an officer.

The center around the train station was on a grid map on everyone's arm. Detail would adjoin the map section to the larger grid of the village. The enlisted man relies on the officer to read maps and make deployment commands based on accurate terrain analysis. The terrain features around the station were adjusted by the train that sat dead still in the middle of the station yard. Observation towers in the yard, six towers, were occupied by observers, and riflemen. There was no nearby hilltop, or ridge that might afford an assault team, forting or cover. The station and the yard were south a draw with a valley exit toward the distant mountaintop mine.

The officers were on top of the command to exit the train. Light infantry squads dismounted the train on both sides. The platoon in the front car placed their fire team in position to maneuver, and overwatch. Success was highly probable with well-trained soldiers and officers who had the most advanced technology in weapons. The exit from the train was a hellride, but after positioning troops, success of the mission was judged by combat service support.

The entrepreneur aboard the train had final notes in his journal.

At the top of the grade. One minute from station stop. 24 hours late. Hardboiled eggs are being passed from hand to hand. Eggs are the soldier's pass. An egg, uncracked will be an identifier. No one expects the eggs to last long. Like the fifty live birds about to be released, hen layers, crated from the U.S.A. Kept alive by ordinary chicken feed and storage in climate control. The hardboiled eggs are meant to identify the good guys, and last just over an hour. The regimental force, and local militia number two hundred fifty perhaps two hundred seventy-five with committed natives. Many victims are native military personnel.

If uncrated at exactly the time of arrival, three hundred times twelve means three hundred dozen eggs were uncrated at the arrival dock for widespread consumption. This was not largesse or charity. The soldier would eat about three eggs per hour. In the next hour he would either give the rest of the eggs away, or use them as a pass with others identified from the train. Everyone off the train would start with the same eggs in order to identify everyone starting at the military aid site, and police action. The eggs were not Easter eggs but they were the most identifiable mark in the first twelve hours of the train's arrival. With soy milk and a large chocolate freight expected, food distribution was very important. This helped establish identity. The village was coming to reclaim its homes and landholding. If the families returning absorbed the shock of losing a village it would be best. Possessions and valuables could be gathered, or landholding rights could be sold. These should go to the highest bidder.

The end of the gold mine was seen as the end of the region. Everyone with the initiative to do so would stay. It was strongly recommended to everyone to let their land come under common ownership. This was intended to be the start of a coalition for collective farming. The area would be filled with farmers with rights to land. The oldest landholder in the area was the owner of the mine. Working the mine required a lease of long term. The term was in dispute. Thirty-seven years ago the last value was taken from the gold mine. On one occasion it had been salted with diamonds, but that was when the town was fully cycling through the plastic plant, where nearly thirty types of plastic containers, pill bottles, and small use bottles were being made. The number can only be imagined. Many times the mine had been leased by short-term owners. They had employed villagers. The region itself was a pasture of sorts, with large areas of herd activity. People ordinarily lived on elevated areas, and visible points of land. The town was at the end of the railhead.

It wouldn't be the villagers that overran the station, but the second train with the backup locomotive pulling up twenty minutes after arrival of the first. Deployment by the peace keeping force was nearly complete, and a section of the first train was already unloading to the station side. When the second train went alongside the first with a distance of three tracks between them, the villagers rushed into the gap between the two trains. From the very outset soldiers, engineers, and trainmen began to pull the villagers towards them with hardboiled eggs. Of the three hundred dozen, most went to the clamor of villagers waiting beside the train. A learning curve was established when it came to how gleeful a villager might be about his return. The lack of food for the villagers meant that a hard-boiled egg was a peace offering.

The UN peacekeepers felt relief and noted the absence of hostility in the crowd surrounding the station. There were nearly eight hundred persons hoping to get supplies, or an overnight campsite in the village. Many would trudge back to the railroad's figure eight. It would seem that everyone transitioned into a refugee camp and the camp was doing well from the standpoint of enthusiasm.

The pictorial field book of the next weeks would reveal a great number of traditions of war had been followed in the region's turmoil. The gold mine was the relic in the scenery. The mine requires a complete history to understand the mine's place and its mystique. The village felt mining carried on local tradition. The pictorial field book would display how swiftly the populous replaced the retreating army. The train began a healthy economic climate again, based on natural resources, and put a limit to the importing of tenderfoots, and unlikely settlers. The army fulfilled the basic training standard of creating a field guide with clever detail and stunning truths. There were many victims with visible marking scars to display.

Many had left at twilight on the day when the ten-thousand-man army occupied the small village of local factory workers. Later, arrived a five-thousand-man militia and regular army force that forced the larger force to abandon the railhead. All vehicles and fuel in the area the fugitive army took with them, after laying a wide path of destruction that included a number of dead. The place of conflict where the most damage had been done by artillery fire and tank fire was the plaza, built around a recently buried water conveyance. That central conflict had been short, desperate, and bloody. The plaza was meant to represent a civil authority in the region.

The more than two hundred forty wedding huts were a massive scene of destruction. Most were pulverized. The visit to this town had been a fatal march for some. Graffiti paints had appeared on brick and timber walls in the plaza water retrieval area. Fires had been built to entertain the invaders with victims. A number of tribesmen, and local, or indentured servants, and mercenary, had been in this force. Four tribes of a known homeland were able to be identified. The larger force had used fuel reserves and put together a fleet of motorized vehicles and trucks, to go onto the sands of the nearby desert. A mistake obviously, to use the desert as a highway. Neither of the two forces had struck a death blow. The one was still advancing in front of the other. Sounds of the moving, militant force was not a funeral procession. The body of the column was marching in double time.

Within two weeks missionary stations dot the area because of the easy access to cabin, and forting supplies. For the next two weeks members of the occupying force, and reserves arrive at the railhead daily. Many people took their exits, too. Members of the occupying force at the railhead were able to calm villagers who were frightened by the exiting army's leader, who said, "It will not be long before they are living in our fields." Within forty years, this small village would grow to the size of twenty-five thousand citizens. The railhead did this.

If you were on the exit train out of the railhead, you were leaving what would someday become an area for the government's mint where the government minted coinage. Within two years of the destruction of the railhead and its resurrection, copper was being mined in large quantities from the near mine. The mint began pressing coins and commemorative medals, engraved with peace and friendship, in the city of Railhead. Imported silver was also being turned into useful products.

A statute erected in the plaza years after the original damage, recognized a brave settler's grave. The statute stood in honor of the wife of Bonaventure Fitzpatrick. After her husband fell, she received his sword and fought like a native warrior. She was large and powerful, and the horse she rode was coveted by natives. They attacked her in order to dismount her, but she foiled them with a slender, French epee. When she wheeled her horse and dashed away, she was pursued by some men, who shouted, "The brave woman. Don't hurt her." Dragged from her horse when they caught her, the woman and the horse became prizes. The woman and horse were later ransomed. This honored survivor of the massacre, among many others, is still living.

Despite all the fear, and children starving from bark soup and surplus grain, which was scarce, many people came to the railhead because tribal noises on the mountains frightened them. Tribesmen from the four tribes were being drafted or purchased as trail guides, interpreters, and hunting guides. That is the nature of the livelihood for the four tribes who had not fled the land for urbanization.

Outside of the movements of battle many experiences brought on near-death encounters. This happened often with stalwart, young natives, engaging their enemies in person-to-person, hand-to-hand struggles. Sometimes these were seen from a distance. Details were carried back by persons within eyesight. Hunters in the area brought dangers. More than likely most were tribesmen, and scouts. The call for militia that comes with confrontation with natives was viewed as a sign to the tribes they should stop all skirmishes. Attacks were repelled by tribesmen if they had support from regular militia forces. At a farewell council of the tribal four, the mercenary tribesmen spitefully decided to ignore the invitations from armed commands and armies and refused to allow themselves to be hired. They decided to send a hollow silver bullet containing a message. The message, a map and a garter made from a skunk skin, displayed a means for escape from the guard house. Many were held there and it was strongly picketed. The four tribe's role in the overrunning of the town and the loss of life that followed was regretted by those clans. Prosecuting warfare would not be part of any of the chief's future interests. Struggles of a different kind, not the type of hand-to-hand struggle offered by warfare, would become more important.

the bike turns in the best ending

Fill Ones Boots is grabbing that advantage.

Sssooo. Fill One's Boots?

CHAPTER EIGHT

Landholding rights that could be sold went to the highest bidder. Land office records indicate that many villagers who returned with the train, left on that train, or left the dangerous, but developing region within a short time. The wedding huts exchanged hands within a short time. Agreements to let villagers live in the destroyed parts of the village with a lease or a rental, were nullified. Most domiciles were not inhabitable without rebuilding.

Any possessions recovered were greeted with surprise. Raiders left little of value. With the plastics factory needing to be rebuilt, manufacturing on the scale that succeeded in this small village was not going to be repeated with the same goals in mind. Planners had new ideas for the plastics factory. The most basic jobs left for those returning was rebuilding the village, or digging and packaging bird guano on the nearby marsh flats.

Carpenters with tools were able to start some work with local landowners who hoped to rebuild. All of the returnees would have taken the job if properly equipped with basic tools, but landowners repeatedly chose single men and women for the job. Families were expected to recover personal property, and leave for the safety of their family. When men heard of the practice of hiring single men and women, some complained. Experienced workmen warned those freshly employed, "How well a hammer puts the nail in, is a product of the carpenter."

Steffie was in the compound finalizing most of the withdrawals from personnel files. She was the key placement officer. A cluster of physical files had been delivered that morning which were an incoming special assignment section, and the general purpose UN files. Nothing sensitive unless you cracked the inner files of superiors who transacted withdrawn files. The UN crew had the most colorful files the administrative aid had ever read. A language distinction was obvious. As Steffie read she considered the blatant nature of file quotations, and comments. They were not commonplace. For example, "elimination of unreliable elements." The information was a view of a recognizable authorized force that would break rules, gain back a free world, and loose themselves on barbarous souls. This was Steffie's vantage point. There seemed to be a syncopation in the paperwork from many countries. In some cases explicit acts of differing factions made choices difficult. File notations pertained to pecuniary interests, and the interests of money. In many files there was pretentious diction. Attempts to add a view of scientific impartiality rather than scientific judgement were obviously dressed up statements made to bias judgement. Throughout it all the normal accents of writing shifted. The writing, false, superior in wit, made the offense, or the defense of it, a chance for disharmony. Timidity and apathy were cast aside.

Differences in words held poetic life. The goal of recognizing the good in every man was attempted. If a file notation should burn in hellfire because the file recommended no one as competent, a request was attached to destroy those documents.

Occasionally a weakness was reevaluated as a virtue. This gave the person, and the virtue a peculiar power. A verbatim hospital statement, or an interview might contain a request for withdrawal. This is from a court transcript accompanied by a fast track for removal by a superior's orders. This transcription was going to be pulled.

"After they administer a shot."

"Yeah."

"Did you know you were going to try to escape?"

"Yeah."

"You mean that's why you got a grounds pass? Where did you stay?"

"At a hotel."

"Which hotel? What was the name of it?"

"I don't know."

Incoming files began to take on a decidedly awkward turn. Practitioners and civil authorities were going to make the location a hospital. Civil and private authorities planned for the region to be connected by the promise of a railhead, a new one, built on a swath through the desert. There was a new flow of incoming information. The flow that would result in an explosion of research space in the surrounding community. The railhead coming from both sides of the desert took away the region's isolation. No army would occupy the region near this burgeoning development, again. Great development in hospital services and science would follow. The community would be a research facility. Not the type of research done on meat-eating dinosaurs. Research on the human heart.

In the planning stages, with a military and overseas financial juggernaut behind them the private research company would introduce incoming medical personnel, teachers, staff, administrative aides, and researchers in contingent sections. Including medical staff, nursing specialists, psychology practitioners, sociology staff, and social workers. Amongst the gathering were banking institutions and laboratories, both private and public hoping to partner in the research facility. Steffie's response to this was "Bring it on." She would rather be an employee of the establishment. Steffie was going to be a civilian. An offer had come in. She had posted it on her desk. It was decorated with a fistful of flowers she had pulled from the edge of the compound during a contemplative walk, then returned to her office and flung on her desk. She had thought sure it would be fun to go to jump school, and tie on that parachute again. That would be practical training and re-assignment. When she received a job offer from the private sector that changed her course of action. The reason was the inducement of a cash offer from a private institution addressing her financial needs at triple what she was being paid in the Army. Security placements put Steffie on the top of the list for advancing beyond ordinary protocol, and understanding the secrecy involved in medical research. The financial offer had literally been made in a boldface uppercase font.

She was spying in her capacity of an intelligence officer on the credentials of incoming personnel, including the following documents. 1) An application for voluntary admission, 2) to whom it may concern letters, be it from a pastor or outpatient psychiatry director. 3) Letters to the court, law enforcement, and private practice psychologists. This responsibility left her with misgivings and compunctious guilty feelings.

Touma Thomaz, in the meantime since he and Steffie had broken off their love affair had been alert, oriented and coherent during his negotiations with the army. The private institutional medical company approached him with renewed offers. The question in his mind discovered the taste of vinegar, and the taste of sweet wine? This was a Bedouin saying. At least it was a transcription. He gave a thumbs down to the offer and refused to call turning the job down with a display of bad manners.

The following document never before published, you will be interested in. Aliases are well guarded in Army files. Revealing an alias might be a spy game. Spies have file stories that read like fiction. Language linked by a code. She read a phrase: "The small snake did not skip off the sidewalk, and the miner kept his step." It followed a mission success message. The message was "The dress going around was a revolving barber pole effect." A collaborator included the note, "He read the year on the coin I was told to add to his pocket change. The year before his birth was a bad omen. The year after his birth was a good omen. He seemed elated." At the end of the file the Subject "Quit" and told the judicial inquiry he would be a moral thinker. Then his aliases were revealed. Miss Fanny Marks. Miss Sober. Miss Phoebe Winecoop. Miss Betty Plumstead. Miss Nancy Willing.

Sam and Genius the lion, were the subjects of several to whom it may concern letters. These originated in the office of Large Type, Touma Thomaz. His idea succeeded in giving the letters a severe angle in emotional worldly-wise. He felt that Sam was educable. He based the evaluation on the opinion Sam had been trained to handle the lion. Touma also wrote that Sam, had an elaborate persecutory delusion. It centered on a plot to harm him. He heard people talk about him. Sam thinks the lion is going to harm him. He thinks Touma is going to harm him. A young lady Sam had been knocking down doors to catch in a face-to-face meeting displayed Sam's social ineptness with her. Touma Thomas recommended treatment for Sam. The way Touma worded the letter it sounded as if Sam requested the letter.

The letters Sam has been writing to a girl were chatty, centering on an escape, an offer of marriage, and a morbid joke he made repeatedly. He had been repeating this joke often. "A baseball team rallies in the bottom of the ninth. A guy at the bar has had a few, and lays his head on the bar, and goes to sleep. The guy next to him says to the bartender, 'This guy here is dead. No one has noticed him but he is dead.' The bartender passes a critical eye over the situation and says, 'He's still breathing. He's not dead.' 'He's faking the breathing, he's dead. But I think you can still make a blood donor out of him.'" Sam's letters talk about leaving every day. He was waiting for discharge. Touma wants him committed. The reason for that is Touma wants to get away with made-up ownership of the lion. Touma has sold Genius the lion to Estaban Dae who is arriving on the incoming train. Touma is struggling with what the truth is and in this case what he thinks the truth ought to be. Sam is hanging on by a thread. Touma has shifted examination of Sam to an incident involving a head wound. The mental weather forecast and the claim that Sam had failed to seek psychiatric counseling was argued. The court record revealed a recommendation that the defendant, Sam, would attain fitness within one year.

Successful therapy and treatment is what is most important. Be sympathetic. At the most base level, at its lowest trough, lies an evaluation of two senses. Is your mental state going to make you educable or, trainable? That is the lowest evaluation. Every mental classification captures a different group of behavior disorders. Advances from there are made by special education. A special education faculty making the world a place of diversity, science, friendship and fellowship can be a prominent success. The son of the honorable holder of many accredited degrees, B.S.E., M.S.E, C.A.S., Ed. D., B.S., A.A.S., might very well hang a plaque in the lobby, or at the front door. Build a 24 hour cold storage meta verse. What happens?"

The waiver of a civil conviction is made selectively in the Army. First and foremost is honor, integrity, and knowing the difference between right and wrong. Raffle collection services of a prospective cadet can come into courtroom on an affidavit, or on a request for an exception, when examining character and honesty. A helpful pastor may sign a letter of support having known him not to smoke, drink or lie down in front of adversity. He could assert the subject will be an asset to other patriots. This would be noted by the court.

Military police can be reasonable when considering language in a civil complaint. Compliance in the case of a missing bicycle. A summons is handed down. The victim will leave a phone message relating cooperation by the offender.

A department of mental health asks, "What is mental health?" Love is thought to be part of mental health. Wellness to yourself, and others. Love letters are rarely found in files that ask questions about mental health issues. One letter, for example, speaks of love and being reunited.

I love you so much. Take me back and I will never be so happy. We never had a major fight and never will. We've had many happy times together. I'd like you to take me back. I wouldn't ever lie to you. I wouldn't be so messy. We will set a firm ground work for communication. Sometimes in the past I've neglected your needs. I feel very remiss in doing this. We would share the household duties, equally.

A second letter; I won't be a rat with a bloody nose. They changed the door on me. The food will be there. My frontal features will not appear to be so aggressive. With the changing doors and the future determined, I love you very much. Again. Love up.

The only file left for Steffie to complete was the exit file on herself. An unusual incident would no longer be a part of her Army file. The material in the file was serious. The subject was her alcoholism and drug dependency. More drug dependency than alcoholism. For Steffie without exposing her own tears this part of her job was pointillism. A work of painting connecting a series of dots by the eye. The big picture made from small dots. At the top of this file for no reason, was a letter from a friend long ago. Tszefanyeh Teppo. Written from a community house it was a letter from a friend. The letter itself starts out all right. "I hope this puts you in your best mood. How's the Tasmanian devil? Mrs. Hoop brought me here." From there, the letter breaks with ordinary. The letter writer cries for restraints and nurse administered drugs. Then addressing Steffie it says. "I sure hope this letter freaks you out, or cracks you up. Sincerely yours, Tszefanyeh." An address is handwritten at the top. This letter says a little more about Steffie than she wants it to. The issue being former social contacts. She wants it destroyed.

As an undergraduate Steffie had been an admirer of Byron the writer. She had written letters to the writer. Then she had them published in a local small press. She posed a high place for her love for him. She wrote he had carried her away as a dragon would and fortune tellers stood guard. This was erotic, flamboyant.

The remarkable thing about the newspaper article under her byline was she translated a passage of Byron. She read and published this quote. "Hespes comesque corporis." Translated, "Friend and associate of this day." From this scholarly quote came revisionists. Her name was noted by scholars. This notation she was pulling from her own file. The erotic newspaper clipping was not going to remain there.

Steffie was interested in a file being worked on by Touma Thomaz. He was creating a file for a Bedouin woman he had met at the desert oasis. He was reaching out to a Bedouin spirit. He hoped to elevate his human spirit. The Bedouin woman saw the art style of pointillism on television in the weather girl's background. The dots and circles, the large curves and small triangles. She was not interested in art. She wanted to be the wife of Touma Thomaz. For this man, Teriasandre y Ateriasandre, understood the meaning of the word ambivalence. She was in love with Touma. He was on the fence.

After coverage of her métier, and profession, Steffie was considering how far her journey would take her. She needed a temporary stay, away. She had been drinking, and smoking chanticleer, and she would like to issue away, nocturnally. She had seen half of what she wanted. The planned mega hospital would to move into the community. As the railroad track coming across the desert was over a dozen miles away, she considered her options. Steffie was going to sign a contract with the hospital administration for triple pay, and corporate housing expenses. In her new job she would work as an executive assistant and lease building machinery, and work site platforms, and accumulate workmen's furniture.

The cash bonus offer was good for sixty days, but it declined from the offer date, to a figure of seventy-five percent, in sixty days. They wanted someone to start right away. Cash incentives were offered along with thirteen weeks a year of paid vacation. Steffie who used golden words and shouted, "best of", had figurative expressions for everything. She was heard saying things like, "Burn it, a fugitive in the universe." She noticed these comments began to raise wisecracks around her. She began to feel the atmosphere around her was distracting. She could hear shouting, running, and fender bumping from rampaging automobiles being parked around the compound's outer barriers. If she waited sixty days to sign into a private contract for the hospital site she would lose a big bite of her bonus. Steffie was considering what to do. She wanted to get that extra twenty-five percent of her bonus. She said to herself, "Three weeks parachuting, in the Army facility and two weeks of travel, and courier assignments. Special agent class." It seemed like it would be worth twenty-five percent of her bonus. The Army had offered parachute instruction, five weeks of social play, community activities, and physical exercise for personal and professional goals. She knew she would tire of self-guided activity and vacation. While not under the influence of sugar, or soda, or coffee, or drugs, or alcohol. That combination for Steffie was her daily melee. With new paperwork being delivered with corporate type, Steffie began to consider how to gain placement, and successful hiring. Plus get a sixty-day delay. She wanted a pantheistic clause, forgiving the sixty days out of service. As if a pandemic delayed bills for telephone and cable service. She was looking for a break in her schedule. She wanted a way to make her due date, the day she would have to pay up, and reenlist in a good job a date in the future. The idea she came up with was to try to do two jobs, and be two people, in the short term.

A simple portrayal of her disassociated self. Most people can't handle it. Using an alias and paying no tax. This came from a delusional sense she felt about having carte blanche with the personnel files. She had toured the files with a free hand and unconditional authorization. C'est la vie. That's life. She wished to accomplish something that would make her feel the inner grandeur for doing the impossible. She didn't like being under pressure. So she shifted some paperwork, produced an old picture, and created documents following her file to New Zealand. She claimed to be from among the tribe named List and created herself as an aborigine. She created both documents and an identity traced to an internet figure who was an aboriginal. Now she was Steffie Toro, from Kekepania, New Zealand.

She was going to change not just in spirit, but in the flesh. In the real sense. Changing each part of her personality and individualistic self. She didn't have to push her beliefs on someone else. She could keep things quiet. Aboriginal art wasn't going to come after. Two beautiful women. Steffie Toro, and Steffie Thom. Two beautiful artists. All so she could get the new employment bonus. Done with mere paperwork and authentic looking reprints. Without a goodbye, or sincerely yours, Steffie Thom became Steffie Toro. She was still able to have healthy thoughts within her changing self. In the first place, the general recognition of alcoholism, and drug dependency were obvious to her. One day Steffie as the victim would parable her recovery to an afternoon magazine talk show. She was able to recognize her alcoholism and drug dependency, which began as the pressure of her work changed her outlook.

The reason is simply this. She was changing the physical universe. Her footprint had become disturbingly critical. She began to make observations. She began to develop an appreciation of the reflection of Mars, the morning star. She settled into a catbird seat and looked at the evening star, Venus. In Steffie's quest for blackness, a Stygian blackness over the documents she was shredding, she paid a price and sought a clerk's fee. She signed documents using an artistic symbol. Two intersecting V's that form a W said, "Hail! Live! Viva!" She printed it, looked it over, finally adopting it as her own. Officially, she could retire her thinking cap. She was still brainy. She would study this part of the universe she had created. Good men and women who followed her would walk in her footsteps and along the same avenues. She however had changed and wanted to become Aboriginal.

Steffie Toro, in order to protect herself was going to claim Athens as her remarkable place of birth, a place where both of her parents had traveled to. Athens, 480 B.C. to 430 B.C., the time of the specimens of ultimate human perfection. Not those early dates, of course, but a realistic connection with the modern calendar. The forger who leaves no trail, versus, the forger who does not know how to spell. Now Steffie Toro had two identities. She was, "Educable, and trainable?" There is a constant census.

sitting in the landscape a lady in fabric

Baby giraffe for me is half a pint.

CHAPTER NINE

No longer would lack of theatrics stop the show. Once Steffie got the elephant on the station siding she was quoted, "I never do anything, in a non-theatrical way." When the elephant rose from kneeling, Steffie carried herself like an affluent aristocrat aboard Alisa the showboat elephant. Steffie Thom, now Steffie Toro, Athenian aboriginal, thought herself in a pretty eye-catching outfit for a U.S. Army Lieutenant. She also wondered how she would look in a three-piece business suit. Atop the elephant she swayed on her new, bone-shaking conveyance.

The job she had undertaken for the private sector hospital had been completed without interference from her duties with the Army. To the Army she was Steffie Thom. For her new employer she was Steffie Toro. She had done research and found a supplier for rebar and structural steel supports which would be part of the building foundation. They intended to make a large concrete "pad" once construction began. Finding a supplier and ordering the rebar was the raft she was making for her new employment. The immediate area was classified a war zone and would not be occupied for eight weeks, by the civilians, workmen, security, police, and villagers. Delivery of the rebar in fifty days meant she could relax, and wait for further instruction compliments of her private employer. Her instructions had been to relinquish her job with a valediction farewell. Take leave with pay.

On leave with pay, she sat astride the elephant making a leisurely stroll toward the rail station. They were in the comfort zone between the two trains. The ground was slippery.

Among the people striding along after the elephant was a young UN voting representative.

The people's right to vote was his central purview. He had a very narrow license of activity. He believed absolutely in self-government. He took a desultory jump when Alisa the showboat elephant took a hop, skip and a jump over an ivory colored casket left beside the track by workmen. Bodies were being placed in caskets. The train had come with wooden caskets. Bodies were being packed in wadded newspaper, another item brought by the train. An entire half carload of newspapers, now nine days past their press date. It had lingered on the siding after rail traffic was stopped, then been attached to the relief train. Newspapers from around the world. One half carload. The other half was construction tools, and a circus size tent.

The pieces of a tent and a stage would reach to the heights of heaven and marriage. The Bedouin bride's father had sent a tent down to the railhead. He was coming for its use in three days. He wanted to see the man his daughter said was part of a think tank. His daughter said they were to be man and wife. The bride's father had a large entourage. Inside the tent a break from sunlight was possible. From the practices of being a Bedouin there was never a break.

The Bedouin bride's father was named Etienne Isti. Etienne was a developer of prize winning homes using advanced technology with voice activated appliances, artificially intelligent doors and high levels of security. Through this trade he had become wealthy. Wealthy enough to claim he was retired. His retirement was possible because he'd found a better way to do things. He was very eager to explain how he did things to his competitors. His business was largely now a development school. With very innovative teaching practices. The school itself was also a tourist attraction. There were some living quarters. Many Bedouin would set up tents nearby, and visit the school.

He still built homes but not the multiple dwelling developments he had earned a fortune doing. His plan was to contact the builders here and discuss the difficult task of a reinforced foundation. He also wanted to know why architectural plans dictated little, or zero, laydown area. He'd spent two years on an anthropology dig near the Grand Canyon after two years at a university in New Mexico. That is where he learned to build homes for the desert. Both culture and architecture are different for the two climes.

Etienne said no to an elephant at the housewarming he planned in Railhead. His daughter, the Bedouin beauty who had embraced Touma Thomaz as her husband-to-be, would be happy to see her father. She had been a courier in the desert during the battlefield displacement. She had been on the cutting edge when it came to television appearances. She was a resource for international news sources, and independent satellite journalists. The Bedouin bride had been an international competitor in the Olympics, competing for Russia. She was third seat on the team bobsled competition. She was superfast and loved to sled. Some people thought she might be the great granddaughter of Anastasia. Her trousseau of special clothing and household items was already prepared. Her dowry, to be handed over to her husband was an amount still under negotiation. She planned a matron of honor. Her best friend was a woman from the tribe. After marriage she thought that place would be taken by her husband-to-be.

Ngongo, the elephant's mahout, was a well-known driver. A mahout will sometimes suffer from misadventure. A death by accident is possible. If this involves the elephant in a legal case, which arouses public interest, often the elephant will be a cause celebre. The elephant's value is overriding in an accidental death. An elephant's importance was high ranking. The mahout on top was a lesser celebrity. He could maintain this status as long as he avoided a mishap. Ngongo liked to make sure Alisa the showboat elephant didn't do anything impulsive.

Striding alongside the elephant, the UN's representative had begun a flirtation with Steffie. Mostly one-sided, he was giving thought to trying to become her beau. His foolish infatuation he punctuated now by yelling up to her. "Howdy, pardner. My name is Tipene. Tipene Stefaniya. I am here to discuss issues that may go into a voting referendum. There is a local proposal that will be coming with the hospital being planned. You'll see. We want to register people in our new community. Register to vote."

Steffie wasn't up to feigning interest in Tipene at the moment. Her broken affair with Touma had left her with very little ardor toward others. Tipene's serenade of sorts was not returned. Trying to keep up with the leisurely elephant, Tipene stumbled over rough ground. Alisa's mahout Ngongo seeing him stumble wiggled his toes behind the ears of Alisa pausing her walk. Catching sight of this Tipene stood in front of the elephant tapping his wrists together. Alisa stood on her hind legs and tapped her front feet in a similar motion. Steffie aboard the elephant was mystified at this communication. Despite her awkward situation atop the clowning elephant, she felt a bit of reverence for Tipene who continued to gesture.

From his tower command position Overview felt the elephant was an opportunity. He could make it out on the field scope and on a video screen. The cameras were motion sensitive. Center screen was the elephant with Steffie Toro aboard. If he could get the elephant to take commands such as "Tah!" for stand up and "Hmet!" for kneel, then he could use the beast to unload the train. Alisa would have to be guided by the trainer, Ngongo. The UN representative suitor Tipene would have to stay out of the way.

Steffie, the parachute specialist was comfortable aboard the large African elephant. Alisa, the showboat elephant had been raised by East Indian trainers. Alisa was an accomplished worker and performer. Her history if brought together from many sources, would make a colorful, warm, story for the boys to tell each other. In this case Alisa was a mother who goes forward for a new career. That is what Alisa the African elephant, raised in India by *kunkis* had written into her own showboat story.

Kunkis are trained elephants. Their job is training other elephants. Elephants to be trained are tied between the *kunkis*. Mahouts lead them to river waters where they are bathed, taught to be social, and learn to bear burdens. They can also discern verbal commands and sounds, usually a cane striking a hard object. Alisa, the African elephant, had done many things including hard labor, then managed an escape and sustained herself by wild foraging. Recaptured, she was domesticated to labor in a lumber camp, then taken to a circus, trained in performance in the tent before crowds, and retired to a zoo. The zoo's trainer made extra money renting her out for show business. She was a veteran of international movies and television. Just past an age where she would reveal whether or not she intended to increase the size of her family, she was a former lumber camp laborer, and now a show business prima donna. Approaching, the age you would find in the life span of a human being. A lady stepping out again.

The same was true of Steffie Toro. Stepping out again. On top of Alisa. The twosome was quite the charming center of attention. Habitually seen from elephants is a shoulder raise where the shoulders are uneven. People will run up to the elephant certain the person aboard will fall off. It is possible the howdah, the canopied seat atop the thick skinned mammal may be level and then again it might not be. People circle the elephant until the giant beast levels its weight and levels the saddle atop. This allows the rider to sit comfortably.

Across the landscape by the train there were eggshells, broken and scattered. There was a new radio station including a temporary tower for public broadcast, and a news information service that was essentially three people who ran the radio station. They also owned a shoe press facility where they could make shoes. The shoe press was an easy install. The news service began at the end of the track, where they posted a large, white fence, with maps and space for others to post information. It was its own kind of a *greenstreak* newspaper. Everywhere along this white fence came trade of some kind such as bottled bond and groceries. There was an outrageous atmosphere surrounding the white painted wall. The vendor stood with his hat (the size of a mad hatter) and said about the half a rail car of newspapers, "The society pages still carry pictures of engagements, and those recently wed." This was to him good cause for a sigh of relief. A great day for the newspaper man meant he would be going back on the train. He said, "I would like to work with kids." The newspapers got shifted away from the track by kids already stuffing their shirts with the papers. Other kids then left the tracks with stacks of charcoal that came on the train.

The radio people interviewed a lot of the kids, and these kids were defined by size, agility, and family. Kids knew other kids. Your family knew that family. Now at the station stop, kids were overjoyed at the circus atmosphere which brought danger even as you stepped out of the way of the elephant. Someone yelled, "Out of the way of the elephant."

Steffie was having a pretty good time atop the elephant. But it was a double date. To make the elephant work, Ngongo, sat on Alisa's neck, stuck his toes behind her hears, and helped direct the elephant, usually with just his toes. Alisa and Ngongo had been together a long time since both were teenagers. Behind Ngongo sat Steffie. She was in the saddle, wooden and cloth, strapped to the back of Alisa. From that burden Alisa wanted less shifting of weight, so she shrugged when Steffie gave a little jump while standing in her seat. She wanted to get off the elephant. Steffie was a top scorer in the Army parachute jump. She wanted to dismount the elephant. Not bungee jump style. She just wanted to dismount.

She wanted to execute a satisfactory PLF. Parachute landing fall. Minus the parachute. There are five points of performance in a parachute landing fall. Feet, calf, thigh, buttocks, and push-up muscle. Falling toward drift is also scored. Steffie had modified her PLF, and called it the "collapsing tower." In her uniform it brought attention to her. Now standing in the seat atop the tall elephant she stretched her legs. Ngongo wiggled his toes behind the ears of Alisa and raised a hand toward Steffie. She came down in the "tower." A satisfactory execution of her PLF. Before jumping from the back of the elephant she said in a lyrical voice, "Dragons, vivid with paint, some say ornate, send me some pocket change." Then a brief moment to relax, then the PLF. Was it a nine point nine? She nailed the dismount for a ten. Ten. From the howdah on top of the high stepping elephant. Alisa, the elephant, was so impressed, she took a bow too. That was the way Steffie rolled.

Overview sat atop a field tower. Overview took a look at Steffie through the field telescope and went back to his original orders. Overview's job was to find out who is choosing to stay, who is weak, who is innocent, and who is not. Quite a task for a job that is rarely filled with endearments.

lady in the mirror-as-Sitt-Fatima

Percussive maintenance with me striking it, to make it work

CHAPTER TEN

"My name is Oliver Overview. The short walk to the ambulance exchange point was a fast realization for me. The walk was brisk and I must say without apprehension that medical evacuation for all injured parties meets our goals. Meeting our goals and being friends is a different realized objective. I have an AOI, I mean an area of interest, and I have an AOR, or area of responsibility. All of the men, women and clergy have an unconditional undertaking in serving the sick, the elderly and the injured. Everyone is using a raised level of human intelligence to make effective the medevac. I mean the medical evacuation. All of the personnel in the PZ, pickup zone, are all within a radius of vulnerability and on standby for a threatcon. That is a threat condition."

Captain Overview was in a special position to place the railhead into workaday hierarchy. He wasn't the top MPC, military pay certificate, but for periodic intelligence he was at the top of military personnel. He had maneuvered everyone under his control, and kept onlookers at a minimum safe distance. He was also being interviewed by two journalists, one holding a camera and the other a microphone. He was being careful about sensitive compartmented information. He was acting modest and personable. He was also scratching his scalp as it itched after a recent haircut. The lady camera operator thought he looked handsome.

The journalists were freelancers. Both were Russian. Their organization's main goal was to identify enemy prisoners of war and identify WIAs, wounded in action. Rebels were stumbling out of the desert and surrendering to UN forces. The journalist's London Bureau was developing a Green Paper that would stimulate comments and discussion. Neither of the two journalists had been unnerved by the sitemap, the situation map and were looking for the general direction of hostilities. Most of the communication between them was semantic gestures. Sign language. The London News Bureau's emblem stood out on the side of the camera. The logotype carried a distinctive cachet.

To some the presence of the colossus news bureau in this forsaken place was earthshaking. To Oliver it was strategic. He needed help on a project that was personal in nature, but needed SERE, survival, evasion, resistance and escape. Both journalists were experienced in E and E, evasion and escape in hostile territory. He didn't want to wear a body camera, but he wanted someone to film the alarm he was going to spread in his aim to create a robust, yet ultimately, humorous fear. He wanted to quail someone who had been bothering him about something. He knew the journalists wouldn't flinch.

His sister had begun murmuring to him nervous that an unusual number of phone calls made to her house in the States were upsetting her household. His sister's daughter had been contacted by a mail order pharmacy that was selling opioids to his niece. She was using and distributing *Coll-isions*, an opioid-based pain reliever. Also, a recreational drug. The calls made over secured lines had grown hysterical in nature, and his younger sister was calling on her older brother for help.

His sister had tried to understand the nature of oxycontin. It was an opioid pain reliever that could cause insomnia. Overview's niece never slept according to his sister. How long she had been using it she did not know. It seemed like months and months. Calls to the house from the mail order pharmacy sometimes came at 4:30

in the morning. If the niece was using it for pain, the drug after using it four weeks creates additional receptors in the brain for pain signals. Stopping suddenly can cause withdrawal symptoms. Overview's sister understood the medical issues. To her these were not meaningful. His sister admitted she still loved her daughter but those deep feelings were changing and her thoughts were under pressure. So she was seeking help from her brother. She wanted an end to the phone calls, and a peaceful home. A truce.

Overview was considering a conplan, a concept plan. What he wanted more was an ROI, rules of interaction. He wanted to meet them on their own turf, and get them in his LOS. Line of sight.

To begin he examined some issues his sister had raised. She researched the nature of sales calls made insistently to her home. She was wearing a knee brace due to a recent fall in her home chasing the phone the daughter held in her hand. None of the calls were abbreviated. Even when the daughter said "No" the caller made it nearly impossible to hang up. They wanted an accelerated sales report. A tacheo-squeeze was employed by the telephone intruder. Complaining calls to the seller's hotline resulted in a complaint from the seller to never call again with burdensome calls of complaint. The names of the callers were always changing. Over time the same voice would change their name. Official calls of complaint to the state's attorney general, resulted in a recorded message. The calls come from various states. Sometimes the same voice called back about cardholder services, or an offer for computer security. The same caller would offer attractive credit card rates, or increased card security. Offers of free prescription fills were also made. Sometimes calls resulted in only silence. These were targeting the person on the receiving end of the phone. Those were annoying. This tormented Overview's sister. This sales approach was using the telephone with intent to intimidate.

It is a criminal offence to repeatedly call someone. Telephone harassment is a form of discrimination. In some cases a maximum punishment of up to two years, and a forty-thousand-dollar fine can be applied. The Telephonic Communication Protection Act is in place to address these issues. The sellers who change numbers make ineffective annoyed calls to donotcall.gov. Complaints are made to no avail.

It is often loud and noisy in the calling room. From there callers sound polite and vulnerable. The callers are usually not alone. They work to develop the uncanny ability to establish empathy. They do not see the sales story as preposterous. It is one told regularly. Together they manufacture spellbinding oratorical skills. Yet, the upper-class language in the grumbling phrase, "Now is the time for all good men to come to the aid of their party" reveals an upstart complainer who is a Johnny-come-lately with pretensions. No chance of that one stealing commissions. Raising a fuss doesn't work.

For his part Overview decided he would employ obfuscation. He thought the journalists would BP. Be prepared. They would be within his CFA. Covering force area. The addresses he had obtained were within the buffer zone for the hostile phone callers. They were using employing mechanized automatic dial computers, computerized, shifting call numbers that convert phone numbers and extensions. Available information on the individual's heights, and weights, and other physical descriptions, were available only as a font size attached to their voices. They formatted phony foreign accents, and played foreign language characters. There were date lines and time sorts, and character keys they hoped would produce sales records. Overview had a clip board of information that he hoped would put him in the right location.

In the case of Overview's sister and his niece, the computer response was a double sort, with both Oliver Overview and his niece's name revealed. The calls began to Oliver. He risked a 90-day supply of antibiotics delivered to his sister's. He was recovering from a bloody training exercise injury to his shoulder. That is what began his responsibility. This was the formula that led to his niece's situation. That began the hostile caller's salutations. What Overview was seeking was parity where both he and the callers would agree to the same even temper and equilibrium. It seemed unlikely that the sender would sign his or her name. Overview was going stand in as a wild card character and all the callers he would organize into a subdirectory. His plan would begin with words not included in the standard dictionary. Foul curses had been made.

That was the kernel of his idea. He was hoping to muzzle confusion. His actions would not imitate a journalist's docudrama about the issue of free speech versus the right to a fair trial. He was going to develop specific cases bearing on the controversy. He would quote his own sources and amplify his own gratuitous violence. That was his pipe dream. Even if thwarted at his worst he imagined the resulting situation would leave him buoyant. He was going to confuse all hostiles, and skedaddle with footnotes. With the journalists in hand he would decamp with videotape. With a self-imposed limit of advance he would leave the opposing platoon in the dark.

Overview as King Kong wanted a rendezvous. Why was this infatuation implausible? About Kong some might be smitten. Overview's torch song would be a serenade. The result more than mere argument. Radiation around it an absorbed dose. More than a positioning of scare tactics were part of Overview's periodic intelligence summary. This was on his mind as were many other things. Overview's responsibilities included the willow-pattern of a wedding.

The wedding between Touma Thomaz and a Bedouin bride Teriasandre Ateriasandre, was originally planned NLT, not later than three days after the arrival of the train. This marriage would be a civil ceremony. Songs and poems were planned. Some spoken and then sung would praise the splicing of the two.

For this celebrated event Overview had cleared work schedules, and enabled the assembling of the tented structure being raised for the wedding ceremony. This was the chance of a lifetime to see the building of a unique temporary structure. On the first day after the arrival of the relief troop train more smaller though no less impressive temporary structures arrived by train. The bride's father was sending work crews and dressing rooms, stages, temporary homes, rickshaws, drivers, blankets, bedding, food, motor scooters, portable showers, cooks, dressers, builders and photographers. The small, temporary city was being built, housed and fed by the wealthy bride's father. Most spoke reasonably good English. The journey to the railhead passed through some very hostile territory. Peace negotiations were hoped for amongst the warring militants in the desert. The bride's father assigned work and then spent most of his day trying to pleasantly pass the time away. All this under an overhead third quarter waning moon.

The daughter arrived from the desert, having lost five large suitcases containing most of her clothing. All of the presents she was transporting to give to relatives, in-laws, and friends were also part of an expedition to recover them. They had sunk in a dry quick sand bed, along with a camel. Some effort was being made to dig them out. Upon arrival, the bride, Teriasandre y Ateriasandre was intimidated by the sight of the heavily armed military guards along every walkway. Some ill-dressed guards seemed to be lounging, and looking bored.

At first the bride-to-be enjoyed the workmanship of all the structures being raised. A metal frame goes up then a vinyl or canvas cover. Then aluminum doors and carpeting are added. As the day wore on she began to tire, and upon a visit to the doctor, who was visiting everyone, and accepting bribes for treatments, Teriasandre was found to have a temperature of one hundred two degrees. She argued for the diagnosis of the hot sun and a ride in a motorized rickshaw. After admitting to having a stomach ache, occasional chills, and pain in her joints, she was taken to the large tent where the ceremony was to take place. A day bed was brought in. Around the makeshift physician's clinic the wedding tent was filled with fascinating works of art decorating four walls and each corner of the structure. The high quality skilled workmanship of the art was an obvious source of pride for workers and construction personnel. The doctor as the center of attention in the room in a beautiful Sari and with short hair, acted as a gracious hostess as her patient lay on the bed suffering at the hands of everyone who offered a home spun diagnosis. The well-educated doctor began to engage in some socializing with workmen. There was conversation among many of the bride's attendants who were present. As alcohol was being stocked for the wedding celebration, some attempted to engage the others in some drinking, but most of the men there had no experience with alcohol. After a short drinking session and some socializing conversation the bride-to-be said she would like to take a nap, and everyone but the doctor retired from the room.

After a short nap Teriasandre awoke and asked for tea. The doctor pours her patient drinks of tea, weak, watery buffalo milk, to be served in a tall teacup. Her traditions meant she served the tea overflowing into the saucer as an act of generosity and hospitality. The bride cooled the tea by blowing on the liquid in the saucer, and then sipped from it. After admitting she might try something to eat, Teriasandre was not able to stomach the dish of rice and string beans she was served. When the doctor took her temperature it was one hundred and three and many workmen came back into the tent all addressing the doctor in foreign language. Only about ten percent of these men spoke English but the ones who did served as interpreters. Some stood by and urged Teriasandre to eat heartily. Their hospitable tones were turned away, and the doctor ordered her patient to be carried to a smaller tent where she would be cooled with ice packed around her arms and beneath her neck. Since the homespun cold remedy of tea and milk hadn't affected her condition something worse than a cold was considered. The prevailing diagnosis was food poisoning, or worse.

After what seemed to be a pause in preparations most people around the wedding city took a recess. The men took it upon themselves to shave in the immaculately clean temporary restrooms that had been constructed. Many indulged in a light meal being served in the brand-new tented commissary. Others went for a tour of the water processing plant, and others just sat and watched the newest travelers and traders arriving by train. More commissioned works of art arrived by train, and they were placed in tents. Traders and peddlers arriving by train also sold small works of animal art. Most were simple elephants, lions and carved wooden giraffes. Many tribesmen were very curious about the hot water showers and western style toilets. Some men got drunk on black market booze.

Men and women were eating, and changing clothes in separate tents. There was great excitement. Ladies retold long-winded tales men had glowingly fascinated them with. Elaborate wedding ceremony descriptions attracted attentive listeners. They were impressed and overwhelmed by descriptions of it all. They could not hear enough about the experiences others had beheld at their own weddings. A new rendition brought by oohs and aahs. Everyone either pressed for answers to their questions or supplied answers to question after question. No detail was too small for the large audience. All the while spectacular gowns were being unpacked and tried on by women readying for the wedding.

Touma Thomaz, the groom-to-be, came down from the area of the mine and the radio towers and was allowed to see the bride only briefly. If she was ill, her recovery was an importance of great magnitude. Touma tried to soft-pedal the idea that she might give him the illness that was affecting her. The aroma of the sick room made him feel queasy. The general feeling was that she must be isolated, and the groom must not take any risks. No one knew if he had a developed immunity to whatever germ had put her to bed. So the men took him for a walk towards the lake and they passed through the many palm trees, and over the short hills along the beautiful lakeside.

As they walked along Touma realized that he had a following which had become quite a large entourage. A small contingent of the men were moneychangers. Touma noticed many vendors had arrived carrying wares, and special goods that were interesting to him. So he exchanged his U.S. dollars for Russian rubles. These seemed to be a common unit of exchange. This foray was exciting. It seemed like a clandestine undertaking. The men stopped walking and waited for him and his vendor to walk alone and make the exchange. Then everyone discussed with him and tried to discover if he had been hoodwinked. They decided he had not. He felt vulnerable and insecure that everyone knew that he had a large amount of cash, both dollars and rubles on his person.

Upon his return to the wedding city he visited the people standing outside the wedding tent. He watched practiced sand painters making symbolic patterns on the ground and in sandy boxes sunk into the earth. These were offered as valuable gifts. Photographers were capturing the art being made by hand. Their gifts were filled with symbolism. Artists approached their craft solemnly.

In the wedding tent, flowers were arriving and the stage was being lit with bright floodlights by professional video and still photographers. Food was being served. One could barely take a bite without being offered more food. A band of musicians began to unpack instruments including a keyboard, a drum set, and brass instruments including a sousaphone, an upright euphonium and a valve trombone. In practice they were producing blasts of non-melodic sound with great force and enthusiasm. There was an area next to the stage for gifts. It was a very fluid scene around the stage.

One of Teriasandre's sisters, the oldest, declared herself in charge. She stated this very clearly, loudly and repeatedly to all around her, that she is the eldest daughter, and as such was entitled to be and in fact was now in charge of all the decisions to be made about everything that going on in the wedding city. The tent was full of women rushing to fulfill her orders. Tea was being served as it would continue to be about ten times a day. Touma decided to stay out of their way and out of the tent. He went outside and bought three orange sodas with rubles. The sodas were being sold by a vendor, and then he bought several wooden elephants being sold by a ten year old boy. He sat and thought about the clothes he was wearing and realized he needed to get to the compound to retrieve his laundry which had been delivered that morning. He noticed some vendors selling containers of water but felt that drinking the water might be dangerous. At a distance he noticed an accident between a man driving a water buffalo and a motor scooter rider with serious injury to the scooter rider and the water buffalo. He thought about taking a bath and realized he wanted to get back to his own trailer apartment in the compound, and get inside for some rest with the door locked by a heavy deadbolt. He looked at the moon and noticed both horns pointing straight down and considered the radical change in either longitude or latitude from the western United States where he had grown up watching it. The downward cusps seemed to empty the reflected sunlit surface.

As he sat he thought how the mosquitos were not troublesome at this time of year. The evening was pleasant and cool. A girl he had not met came from the side of the tent and handed him a single, folded piece, of flimsy paper, thin and blue. It was glued together at the ends. After opening it Touma read the red letter text without any idea who had given it to him, or who had sent or written it. It read: "Saints have adored the lofty soul of you. Poets have whitened at your high renown. We stand among the many millions who do hourly wait to watch your pathway down. You, so familiar, once were strange. I tried to live as of your presence unaware. But now on every street, on every side, I see your straight and steadfast signpost there." He considered this noblesse praise, and thought more substantively about the coming pageantry of his approaching wedding than who had written it.

black sand on the mountain walk

Tie

Engage notes of the same pitch

CHAPTER ELEVEN

Estaban Dae is on his way to the gold mine with MREs, made ready to eats that arrived on the train. He is not alone. He brought Sam with him who was drifting toward an escape from the camp. Estaban hadn't yet told Sam that Genius the lion was going to be outbound on the next train. Estaban wanted him along while Genius the lion was being transported to the train station. The two left him in his feeding cage in the compound after planning this trip to the mine. Estaban brought food and supplies to the compound to check on the condition of the predatory wild lion. Touma and Estaban were banishing Genius to a zoo for money to be made in the transaction. The lion was going undergo a change. In the new lifestyle zoophiles would love him. If Genius would put in an encore as the foolish cub again that would earn the zookeeper's infatuation. Genius the lion was the biggest business deal Estaban had going at the moment. The long trip he would accompany him on would leave Estaban with cash. That would change his business model, and he would aim for bigger trades.

Estaban wanted to thank Sam and didn't know how. Then again it was possible Sam would not appreciate the offered thanks at all. Sam was en route to the mine with Estaban because he knew something about government common law. The mine's royalty contract was in dispute. More than one party had a claim to mineral rights, and the owner, an English Lord, had pitted the forces of two native tribes by promising both could be a partner in future ore rights. Current royalty interest for the holders was a seven eights interest during production. The Englishman was left with one eighth as his part. To him this was a deadletter law. It was valid under his contract but he no longer wanted it enforced. A possible plaintiff, he wanted to dispense justice in his own way. That alone wasn't enough. He was causing trouble. Native tribesmen he was sending were planting totems around the property, and scaring workers. Sam called the place Black Acre. Due to all the trouble. Estaban was on his way to encourage the mine's residents to agree to a purity contract. If negotiations were successful they would restore the mine and leave. The present owners might agree. Of late they had been introducing inexperienced buyers into the mine who in the figurative sense were examining the diggings in the dark.

The sole military escort was sitting in the back seat of the all-terrain vehicle, an ATV. He was a native militia man who said his name was Cardinal Octillion. Sam and Estaban both knew he had made up his name to go along with civilian attachment to the military militia. An octillion is a one followed by twenty-seven zeros which he thought would classify him as a significant descendant of a branch in his family. He was educated about phases of the moon and claimed a point in the heavens is where his tribe originated. Pointing to stars he would provide entertaining detail on the names of constellations and planets. Other than his militia attachment he was still very much a native. He coveted everything the mine promised. Riches and territorial authority. He was armed to the teeth with both native and military weaponry. Going along solely as protection he wouldn't be involved in negotiations. He trusted no one.

The Row Shell New York ballad "Lizzy the Dove" was blasting from the sound system in the ATV and Cardinal was enjoying it. Estaban had brought along a *meta cassette* handed him by Touma Thomaz at the compound. Cardinal knew a great deal about the mine from childhood experiences. He had been to its very depths. The famous place to others was still a subterranean mystery. He hoped to get down into a well-guarded chamber he was familiar with. There he could carve an assay from the central tree, the supporting structure remaining in the middle of an otherwise sculptured, vacant room. In some places chipping away at a high-grade assay would be very dangerous.

Touma had given the okay for Cardinal's trip with Sam and Estaban, but warned both he was a tribesman. He not only knew the mine, but likely wanted to work inside it again. They should expect him to be a renegade and look to double-cross them. Sam knew Cardinal and was hoping to trust him. Each time Sam turned back to look at him in the back seat he appeared to be sleeping as they bumped along the uneven road. He looked asleep but was awake and bouncing along the road excited by all the possibilities that went with a trip inside the mine, given credit to his character. He felt like a yearling goat in advance of his tribe and was clicking his heels together.

Cardinal had on one occasion been given a training session on the supersize earthmover the mine's operators kept on standby at the top of the mountain to move mine excavations. Huge piles sometimes yielded auriferous metal. The single training session on the machine stayed with him and he was wondering if he could get behind the wheel of the mechanical monster. Then Cardinal would show what kind of skill and intense ambition he hid from most people. He considered himself first and foremost a person of his tribal nation. That was his ambition. He would be prospecting along the English titan's entire gold banket.

Sam was quiet and wondered what role he was expected to play. He joked with Esteban that neither could count the number of tattoos Cardinal had above his neck or his waist. Both areas of his muscular torso were exposed by the gown he folded over his shoulder. They tattoos seemed like a single collected pattern of dots, circles and wavy lines. They displayed a story of his wives, his life and the lives of his children. The remarkable display on his body told a story of his kills of a lion, a leopard, a wild boar, a water buffalo and a crocodile. Most natives were wild animal killers and did not consider themselves poachers. They would kill to eat and they would kill to sell wild beasts for bounties, and hides.

Sam had packed his things inside his room at the compound but never intended to return there. He wanted a new life. His old possessions he left on his bed. He also unpacked his best suit of clothes and laid them out on his bed. They were the avatar modeling his former self. They embodied a way to help him out of a difficult situation. Leaving a decoy might give him a little more travel time if they searched for him after he disappeared. He wanted freedom from their purpose and the direction they were herding him toward. His own plan after evasion he would invent. For his first destination he would chase down his own love letter, a billet-doux, which hadn't returned an answer. This was in the back of his mind. Meanwhile he focused on the task ahead. He would tour the mining property and help Cardinal and Estaban feel comfortable in the tough situation there. What was ahead would emphasize objective feelings about occupational hazards of the foolhardy kind. These dangers would leave him in his own pitfall.

As Sam navigated through his plans and feelings he realized he needed to find his bearings. The mood he was maintaining was brittle. He noticed Cardinal was keeping to himself in the back of the ATV, and not engaging in conversation. He didn't offer information on the roadway when they pulled off to avoid boulders in the road, or talk with Estaban who kept up a one-sided conversation. Estaban thought the mine was an antiquity. It wouldn't yield an El Dorado of wealth he said with regret. He bewailed this excursion. From the back Cardinal flashed a rueful smile. When Estaban asked him if he thought the mountain's plateau had washed down during a great downpour of rain that occurred ten days past, Cardinal shifted in his seat and his reaction was a backlash of hostile observations. The rain was controlled not by channels cut into the mountain but by forces of nature. Man could not domesticate the weather and the mountain. Why should they bandy the possibility? Just wait and see the condition of the mountaintop and the mine. The silence that followed was only punctuated by the wafting of a pungent aroma of onions. His fusty body aroma was peeling off him like layers. The smell and silence permeated the ATV for a few minutes.

Again Sam focused his mind on his own plans. He knew Cardinal was not dimwitted. When he looked backward toward him he saw Cardinal had slipped a red cap over the top of his head. He turned to the front, and to the back again and felt a sense of disorientation while he looked at the long body of the native in the back seat. His body looked tense, though his face carried a serene expression. The canvas bag that hung from Sam's shoulder contained his food, a cache of clothes and a small club he intended to use for killing fish. Large ones he might catch if he needed to travel by foot. Line and hooks he kept on his belt. He was no match for the fighting skills of Cardinal. The tension was making hackles on his neck rise so he decided to open conversation in the vehicle among the three. At first his voice was only a rasping sound then he began to put into words a story to break the tension. At first his voice cracked but he then began to vocalize in a throaty, resonant voice. The story was not about him, but one he had heard over and over again in the compound by an incarcerated prisoner. Tragedy had befallen operators of the mine. There was a bloody standoff characterized by human suffering and the possibility of revenge and retribution. So the members of the compound put a survivor of the tragedy into a jail cell and forced him to tell, and re-tell his part in the events. Sam had heard the story again and again. The biggest change to the story he began to tell was he told the story as if he were the person in the story. He told it in the first person like he was part of the tragedy. He thought about it for a minute before he began and wondered if this was his dark side. He relaxed his demeanor and thought about the gamut of emotions he would be expressing. He considered the possible overwrought surge of emotions in the two other men in the ATV. So he adopted a relaxed posture. He hoped his dark thoughts might embolden the two men in the salvage mission they were on. They were an envoy to recover human assets. They had embarked on a mission. At the top they weren't in chaos, or in panic. At the top of the mine operators sat on the summit of the human connection to greed, envy, violent dispute and disputed claims of ownership. They also had enough courage to quickstep to a civilized outpost if a risk situation turned against them. The men had human perceptions, strength, understanding of commerce, emotional balance, philosophical ideals and scientific understanding. These are real human personifications. To attribute human characteristics to gold was a pathetic fallacy. Mining was a science. Gold had changed the way men looked at each other since it was discovered and made a symbol of financial strength. This doesn't explain the luck, good and bad, surrounding gold. To understand this could save Sam from punishment that could follow after telling his story. He was taking a risk by placing himself in the central part of the story he was going over in his mind. It was a lie to put himself in the center but he was going to bask in the story he could create. So Sam shifted the attention of Estaban and Cardinal to himself.

"I remember when the Tzefanyehs took over the mine. A whole family bought the leasing rights without seeing it. Maybe they inherited the lease, or won a trip there or, I don't know. There were six people. Three girls, a mother, father and a boy. A little boy, the girls were teenagers. No one was working the mine. It had been abandoned. When the family got there, a lot of stuff was there, and the elevator worked, there was a good-size slag heap, the lanterns still had kerosene in them. But it was winter. The days were short. It was cold, was dark early and the place was deserted. When they got to the mine there were no workers. No miners. They hadn't taken off because nuggets were falling out of buckets and out of the elevator. This is a hard rock mine. You have to crush the rock, then sift the remains. Air hammers have to get air into hoses with air pressure. Someone at the top keeps track of who is at the bottom. The dust and dirt you walk through just in an elevator trip means you have to wear a face mask, body protection, air filters. Some guys won't go down without oxygen tanks. Then oxygen tanks sometimes overheat, or leak, or just run out of air. They get too hot and they can explode. Mr. Tzefanyeh, Mr. Z was okay but working the mine was a tough day. He spent all day but didn't find a seam. He was swinging a hammer, and pounding a chisel. The little boy stayed in the elevator, and kept an eye out for his dad. They came up and you could see little smears of gold dust on them but those gold smears were like flour. A little here, a little there. They stood in the firelight and the mom and her girls would be so happy at the shiny spots on them. But it did not amount to much. You couldn't accumulate anything of value.

"They didn't like being down in the elevator. At the top the mom and her girls worried about the metal cabling that lowered the elevator, how the generator worked and if it still had gas. It took so long for them to get down to any of the levels. They worried about them getting back up. Mining without workers isn't easy. They had come so far. After a day and a half they wanted to go back. Mr. Z was thinking he didn't have the resources. No workers and just his own hammer and a chisel. They had made the trip, but their dream, just an uncommon fantasy was over. They had lived a part of their dream. But it wasn't going to make them rich. The girls at the top had better luck working the excavation heap. They were in the light and they sat there all day. Still they got only a tiny bit of dust. Gold dust. They were afraid of wild beasts, and at the top of the mountain they could see far off. They could hear screams the first night. They didn't know from where. They realized they were the victims of self-deception. The place they spent the first night was the office. The bunkhouses smelled like men and reeked of old food and the nearby outhouses. One of the girls was angry that she was working with her hands in dirt.

"I got there the afternoon of the second day they were at the top. They had helicoptered in with supplies for a month. Food supplies and two oxygen tanks. But that was it. They hadn't been told that everyone had run off. They walked a mile from the helipad to the mine then walked back and the copter was gone. He was supposed to come back in three weeks. The radio tower had been damaged by native workers when they left. So no one knew about them.

"I came from across the desert, around the edge of it. I was alone and thought I could make it to the mine in three days. I did but the place had only the Tzefanyehs when I got there.

I didn't know it but I was being followed by tribesmen. The story of the mine being abandoned was being told in the refugee camp. I thought I could get to it. I did but a fifteen-man group of tribesmen were following me. They came across my tracks and were behind me. At night once I noticed their fire. I stayed on the sand. It was farther than I thought. They had rivals. The tribe who left the place abandoned before the Tzefanyehs came. They thought they should come back and work it for themselves. They had other parts of their tribe attack the mine. It was deceptive. The tribesmen who had been working there were like a Trojan horse. After the attack they left with the attackers to go back to their village and wait."

At first Estaban and Cardinal stiffened their postures at the sound of Sam's voice. Then each began to make short comments in the midst of Sam's story.

"Bad luck," Cardinal said.

"Expectations and the reality of," said Estaban.

You're an explorer. Banging in that chute of gold is not a nightmare. It is worth the effort, for kings. I am drawing on my king's right, like Columbus, sent by kings."

Both Sam and Estaban both turned in their seats to look back at Cardinal, then turned back toward their road.

"Utopia isn't dug from the earth," said Cardinal.

This raised the hackles on Sam's neck again. Estaban tensed and leaned against the inside of the door of the ATV.

Then Sam continued. "The first day I got there, they were aggressive toward me. They wouldn't let me down in the mine. I could tell this wasn't going to be easy pickings. The girls chased me from the slag heap. You could get the color on your hands. I knew where I was. I had found the place, and it wasn't going to be a payday. So I snuck around when they weren't watching me. I looked where I could. I tried climbing down the elevator shaft, but that was a big mistake almost going to be a much bigger mistake. They knew what I was up to. The first night we saw the tribesmen's fire halfway up the mountain. After that they started talking to me. They were scared and wanted to leave. When I told them how I got there, walking along the desert's edge, they said they couldn't do that. They thought I had brought the tribe to them. They didn't trust me. Down there I told them, come face-to-face, they do not guess mayday, this-red palace train, exceptional faces, crown castle, one clap, a shout, in one of the shacks. The tribe had riflemen and hatchets, spears, and might release dogs. The Tzefanyehs had two rifles, two pistols and about three hundred rounds of ammunition. The tribesmen would draw their fire. And that's what they did. The first night I went out into the dark and met Estebe. He was their leader. Mr. Z and his wife fired on warriors who were firing their weapons in the air. The Tzefanyehs used about one hundred ninety rounds. They kept them firing by lying in a trench and moving and shooting. That night Tzefanyeh counted his bullets. Just over a hundred. When I met with Estebe he said three men from the tribe were wounded. That made it a mistake for both sides. I was scared. He knew who I was. He'd seen me in the refugee camp. He said they had followed me after I told the doctor I was going to the mine. The doctor told me not to go. Then a few more people knew. Estebe was worried because his rivals with their king were going to come back. He said there would be *sang et carnage*. It was up to me to leave. He didn't care if I took the Tzefanyehs with me, or not."

At this point Sam stopped talking, and Estaban stopped the car on the last pullover before the top. He got out and walked over to some bushes, and Cardinal got out the other side for a bathroom rest stop. Sam sat in the ATV feeling embarrassed and still trying to recall what the man in the detention had recalled. He had said the next day the attack became more realistic. There were coordinated moves toward the building the Tzefanyehs were firing from. But the firing from them was sparse. The natives knew they were near the end of their ammunition. Sam sat in his seat and remembered how in a surprise all the natives suddenly disappeared. There was firing down the mountain. Estaban and Cardinal got back in the ATV. They hitched up their seat belts and Estaban drove up the steep part of the drive toward the top of the mountain.

Estaban looked over at Sam, and in a hard voice said, "So you were there when they got killed?"

Sam looked over and said, "No. No. The two tribes started fighting down along the mountain. Estebe's people had the high ground, so they fought into a standoff. Fighting stopped when Estebe and his men kidnapped, took prisoner the rival king. They broke through or something. This caused a customary stop in fighting. Then they either barter, trade or funeral the king. I don't know. I never found out what happened. It was easy at that point to convince the Tzefanyehs to run down the other side of the mountain and head for the desert. They were almost out of ammunition, and they backpacked some food. I know for a fact they made it to the refugee camp. So did I. After that they blamed me because Estebe had followed me to the mine. I helped them get out of the camp, but after that I never saw them."

Cardinal leaned forward in his seat when Sam stopped talking. He simply leaned forward over the seat, looked at Sam and leaned back again. Sam stopped talking here, and Estaban still driving said nothing. They pulled onto the top plateau next to the mine, stopped the ATV and got out.

Cardinal stepped out and said over the hood of the ATV, "Un sonido corto intermitente le indicara le finalization sin previo aviso."

Estaban nodded, and headed for the elevator operator. He said back over his shoulder, "Para obtener mas informacion comuniquese con Sam."

Cardinal smiled and said, "Bien."

man on a mountain

Boiling the Ocean, the task long, result little, or none.

WHAT DID YOU SAY? "Boil the ocean, the talk long, the result little, or none.

CHAPTER TWELVE

Overview had written his sister to discuss his career in the military. Most of his handwriting was filled with pleasantries. He did not want to stir up further agonies in her. Activity at the railhead was exciting. Exclamations cast aside new demands for officious role playing by him. There were no enemies of the joyful, festive atmosphere. In the dominion of the wedding preparations ladies seemed to be walking on air. The men exhibited cheerful mental states aided by wine, women and tobacco. It was a catchment area populated with children, young and old, at the new railhead. A tent was devoted to classrooms, with tables and chairs for children of all ages assigned to studies. They didn't seem to mind and would run out at recess and find new temporary structures going up with new people, and private areas for play.

On Overview's mind were the social distinctions and diverse nature of new arrivals. He was preparing to conduct a tactical exercise to support the whim of his sister. His tactical plan would incorporate training exercises and a tactical objective. He was going to employ a combat service guide by answering three questions. Where am I going? Where am I now?, and, How can I best get from where I am to where I should be? Around himself he saw very few people thinking along those lines. He saw a social atmosphere that left him fatigue par le voyage. He was tired from his journey. The ambitious event he found pleasure in at the moment was a soccer game at the edge of the lake. The grass was new and players enjoyed their showcase exhibition of the game. The grass was slick. The players joked about it and said it was "fait avec des bananes." Made from bananas. No one was using the alpha rhythm of their brain. Overview was apologizing to himself for imagining new names to call newcomers. Most people arrived holding a status symbol invented to put them into a trajectory that was upwardly mobile. Everyone seemed to be adopting a persona. The socially awkward teenager was a hobbledehoy. There were gadabouts and civilities. He enjoyed little fraternization among people who would further his objectives. His time at the railhead was near an end. So he cooked up a new game plan.

He began to think like a gamer. He sat at his desk in the compound and could hear individual raindrops on the roof. He put on a headset and listened to a Russian balalaica seven piece band. Touma Thomaz had played it loudly in the compound once. That set off a massive storm of criticism. He had been remonstrated never to do it again. It was confiscated by General Stevy Thomasine, then handed over to Capt. Overview. This would be his first examination of the music. It set off a soul-searching self-inquisition in Overview that left him stunned. It moved him to consider a fast travel training period, and then a punishing practical objective. He needed to create characters of the two Russian journalists and see if they would earn soldier's capital with him. He would try to mend his sister's niece. The opponent in this match, the callers who had frustrated his sister's eagerness to erase the bingeing her daughter was doing, were the pharmacy's callers. They seemed to have an arsenal of zombie long-distance lines, and well-rehearsed operators. Overview first thought of disguises. Togas or frock coats. The habit of a friar. An African dashiki, or a Japanese kimono. Maybe just an ordinary parka and dungarees. The Russian music was making him think of the cold. The music was very, very Russian. Very plaintive and lively.

In the balalaica band the accordion player is the star. He's supported by a guitar, two three-stringed balalaicas, a male and a female singer, plus a glockenspiel. The glockenspiel looks like a ram's horn and sounds like an oboe. Ten thousand rubles for the band can buy plenty of enjoyable musicianship.

Overview was prepared to openly thank current mine workers for their individual efforts. The owner and governor of the mine didn't intend to offer further largesse, or generosity. Overview sat at his desk listening to the music and studying maps. He was mentally preparing for his breathtaking plan. He took off his epaulettes and considered putting on his civvies. Both the Russian journalists spoke very good English. They arrived early at the railhead each day, and made people feel good. They set up a small table and boiled water on a portable stove to make their own tea. They offered people steaming, store bought, cup-a-soup. Neither one wanted to visit the gold mine which they said went halfway to Hades. They were performance oriented. One or the other, Chefo or Kiwini, was always on the move, taking pictures, or talking with people. They sometimes made ungrammatical use of a word. But they always kept trying new phrases. The two Russians had a proud history. Chefo, whose mother was Bulgarian, and whose father was Russian, emphasized traditions made long ago in his homeland. He was compassionate and careful not to scoff at anyone even if they gave him an occasion to do so. Kiwini, whose mother was Hawaiian and whose father was Russian, was a graceful and feminine photographer who was well brought up. She was forthright but not forward, always friendly and courteous.

Chefo spoke very good English and had been a Cadet in the Naval Academy, and an officer in the Russian Navy. On occasion he would tell his favorite story. His favorite story he told like a Socratic irony. He would give details on the Alexander Column in St.

Petersburg, a monument built to commemorate Russia's victory over Napoleon in 1812. While he did this he would praise the crowd around him as he told the story, then undermine their ability to answer questions about the phenomenal monument. It was a single piece of stone 147 meters tall. Massive and weighing six hundred tons he made light of his own ability to understand how it had been transported and erected, then Chefo would boast of his own knowledge of the mortal strength of Russian men and horses. Like Socrates he would ask questions and offer no answers except to swell his chest and pose like as statute.

Kiwini met Chefo on a bargain tour boat ride of the Neva River on the northwest corner of St. Petersburg on the Gulf of Finland. The tour ride lasted four hours and gave a view of the three canals of St. Petersburg, plus the slough around Peter and Paul's fortress, and included a swimming session in the Gulf of Finland. There were large flocks of seagulls, several large ships and many small boats. The boat ride passes near the St. Nicholas Church of the Resurrection. The Cathedral was built in 1881 on the spot where Alexander II was assassinated. The Cathedral was built with money collected from peasants from all over Russia.

Kiwini and Chefo met during the White Nights of winter when sundown is after ten o'clock, and darkness does not come until after eleven. The sun in the winter remains just below the horizon creating an all-night twilight effect.

After Kiwini and Chefo became friends she followed her rule, "Tell not your dreams but to intimate friends." Chefo enjoyed with her more than a swim in the ocean, and her hobby of visiting and photographing ancient castles. Their romance led to his feeling he held the key to the city in many fortresses and towns. In their first adventures they often munched on ice cream bars sold on the streets by babushkas. Nikita Kruschev experienced ice cream bars sold by street vendors when he visited America in 1956. He told reporters that he wanted to have them for the people of Russia. He was successful since ice cream bars packed in dry iced are widely available in Russia, with street vendors doing a brisk business.

Lastly, Chefo who was extroverted felt he and Kiwini shared Russian middle class values. Both followed a very good rule. In your apparel be modest. Keep to the fashion of your equals."

After they were together and grew comfortable with each other they shared an apartment. Since the breakup of the U.S.S.R. all apartments belong to the people. There is no rent to pay and water is only five dollars a month, even though it is not safe to drink that water. In Russia the government tax rate (sales tax) is twenty-three percent but other taxes boost the rate to ninety percent. The clans charges fifty percent so many businessmen ignore the government taxes in order to make a living after paying the Russian *Clans*, composed of former communists. There were many rules Chefo and she would have to follow. Many they were not aware of.

So they planned a travel expedition out of the country. First to Finland then to London. Traveling first by train, near the border, the train was stopped. A big argument occurred in the corridor outside their compartment. Some passengers were required to leave the train because they had too much baggage, and new passengers were coming aboard. Fortunately Chefo and Kiwini only had one big wheeled suitcase and a backpack so they didn't have much of a problem. The argument may have been politically motivated, to dispute between clans, *slavic steppe* passengers *aye* bank paying person, or persons aboard the train. They were lucky and stayed together again.

Overview built a plan for his special assignment that included the two Russians. There would be obstacles to navigate, but that was the easy part. The callers depended on the fact the recipient would never have a face-to-face situation with the insistent, harassing, or smart-aleck caller. They felt immune to threats or pleading. They could get away with any attitude with the addressee. Overview needed to develop a plan that would make the callers need to meet with him. A face-to-face situation identifying the anonymous caller. The person getting the unwelcome calls wants to recuperate and return to good health. On the end of unwelcome calls the receiver sometimes rallies a threat. Insistence of the caller has led to the reaction that is an expression of illness. A face-to-face situation might accomplish little. Giving offense and fright could reconstruct new goals. The addressee might lose the caller's respect, even if there was little. The receiver on the phone might lose self-respect. But damage is done to the relationship. The order of things has changed. More than anything the face to face encounter says, "I'm mad as hell and I'm not going to take it anymore!" The entire affair is choplogic.

That is the trademark for nearly all face-to-face encounters. Overview recognized this as he prepared a plan. So he was careful and utilized recognizable resources. He also added technological advances. He planned it like a video game. Just like a video game the outcome is never guaranteed.

To begin with he ordered a payment account that was represented by a credit card number. The card was issued by a black market service that conditioned a payment two years from the date of use. The credit card does not pay for two years. The interest rate on the card is thirty-three percent for the holder. While most credit cards have a maximum amount this card has a minimum amount starting at ten thousand dollars. Collateral is required. Overview faxed a copy of his automobile title, a 1965 Ford Mustang, the same year a Ford automobile won the Indianapolis 500. Ford was used to winning contests. They won at Daytona in 1963. The design of the Mustang holds a Tiffany award. Overview's car was an original restoration in a Detroit dealer's showroom. He faxed pictures and the deal is struck. The car was valued at eighty grand.

Then he called a health club operator he knew in Miami. He was *Slavic steppe*. Overview spent furloughs in Miami and had over the years maintained a club membership leading women's personal defense classes at the club. He avoided professional static by never taking direct payments. He had captivated the owner's attention because he would lead the young and old, babushkas and adolescents, in rounds of banshee-like defense. Then he provided scoring for his genies. His plan was bigtime. He would buy a big supply."

After some discussion with the club's owner, and the promise of continued classes and a ride in a '65 Mustang convertible, the club's operator says he would help dispense better bingo dots for men. Using a term of poetry that these men were still making heroic couplets, the operator laughed and said he would help Overview and dispense the "macaronic verse."

Overview recognized too, that he was a vigilante. But that did not stop his coordinated dragnet. He needed a disguise, and a ride. An airplane ride that was a classified reaction to revitalizing the Cold War. To some people the two Russian journalists were technically not the good guys. You might be able to say their motives for being at the railhead were unclear. This is an attitude that was long dormant. The railhead would soon be a research center funded by a well-known pharmaceutical company. A strategy to cross-play the Russians might turn out to be a stunning maneuver. That could be a pretty standard first-person experience for Overview. He would hold them together and put them on his side. Picking them as his team was a major part of his plan. He would have to use considerable charm with them both.

He decided to go see Steffie Thom who was back in her office in the compound. The relief train's arrival had been a success. Tomorrow was the original date for the wedding ceremony. It had been delayed for three days due to stomach illness affecting the bride-to-be. When Overview stepped into Steffie's office she was wearing a chiton, the loose woolen tunic worn by women in ancient Greece. Her Hellenic profile reminded him personal friendship shouldn't interfere with the request he was going to make. He couldn't help but notice the beautiful gown and matching hat, eyeliner, and scarf and shoes. She blushed, as her Athenian dress matched the couple's party. Everything about her was the same shade and would fill in the color of the assembled multitude. She felt close to the earth. She had risen from greenstreet to blossom. Now she helped others search for earthtones.

She was wearing a handsome gown she had gotten from the ladies in waiting. They were enjoying their roles in the intellectual symposium at the wedding tent. Much was being said about the delay, the everyday preparations that were more magnificent, and the celebrated bride's father who was enjoying the company of peasants and would make this activity a resounding success. The delay was just part of the tale.

Steffie had written letters of the Greek alphabet on a blackboard in her office. Across the top of the board she had also written the word "Toro." Overview didn't understand the significance of either the Greek alphabet, or the word "Toro." Those things slipped his mind when he asked Steffie, still Steffie Thom to Overview, for a relief mission flight to the States. It wouldn't have to be secret. Steffie was busy building a bag of tricks in her war against reassignment and re-conscription. She shrugged when he asked would she send him and his team of Russians on a debriefing mission back to the States. The Russians had seen and photographed plenty of scenes of the battlefield. He was a Captain. She was a Lieutenant. She was busy making souvlakia at her desk, the Greek shish kebabs made from meat and vegetables then cooked over charcoal. She was already warming briquettes in a grill outside at the bottom of the stairs.

Steffie surprised Overview when she said, "Will you be my date to the wedding?"

The answer he thought would get him a plane ride. "Yes," he said. "And I will supply you with a dowry you can give to the bride."

Steffie looked up at Overview when he said this. The husband-to-be was Touma Thomaz, her ex-boyfriend. A slight disappointment in her eyes faded. Instead of Touma she thought of reconciliation in her relationship with Overview. They hadn't spoken much since the glass throwing incident. She turned and tapped the blackboard behind her above the Greek letters, and said, "Alpha male, beta girl," and went back to preparing kabobs. Delighted he went out the door and back to his own office.

Once inside his office he made an international call that got him a postal address at an upstate New York mail center. He paid for a box number with a money wire directly to the commercial address. He registered it in the name of "Toro Apothecary." Then as he sat at his desk Steffie knocked at the door, and asked if he would like to join her for kabobs in the compound. They stood on the top steps outside her office eating from plates balanced on the handrail. They both remarked the smell of meat in the compound wasn't the usual problem it had been. Genius the lion was on his way to the zoo.

The lion was caged after taking the trip on the trailer Stavros brought back to the compound. The cage sat in a roped off area near the station, and the lion sat waiting for the return of Estaban from the mine. After a day of waiting and being a spectacular attraction for people arriving and waiting at the railhead, the bride's father decided to have a larger cage constructed, and moved the lion over next-door to the wedding tent. Genius couldn't win in an attempt to return to nocturnal wanderings. No one thought he was in the least bit domesticated. The ruthlessness of commercial activity put him in his personal cage. He was just potential turnover. Exchanging cages was an event that became a notorious drama.

The new and larger cage made for him was constructed from some cut lumber, and medium size tree trunks. There was a top to the cage. It was driven with stakes into the ground outside the wedding tent. The door on the small travel cage with the lion in it swung inward. The door on the wooden lumber and tree trunk cage had a door that swung outward. With the door open to his small cage the handlers thought he would escape into the larger cage when the door was open. But then the door sizes didn't match. He could turn and leap out the door of the larger cage, and over his smaller one.

Plus, the large cage's door would remain open until the small cage was pulled away. A solution was found. The door to the large cage was reconstructed so it also swung inwardly, and was smaller at the top so both doors would match. The entire ordeal lasted for hours drawing a larger and larger crowd. Everyone tried to help and give advice on the large wooden cage's construction. This exhausted the lion, and gave Genius plenty of opportunity to frighten people within a few hundred feet. By the time it was over the scene was like a diorama with exhausted people and the lion begging for sleep. Lions do not hibernate but by the end Genius was wandering along the edge of the cage brushing his mane against the tree trunks and lulling everyone to sleep with huge yawns. Escape was on his mind and he turned the event into a vigil. He was the sentry on the inside of his kingdom. He was a cunning wannabe refugee.

Stavros was acting as master of the station, and in charge of the huge inventory arriving every three or four hours. These were special cars loaded with wedding foodstuffs, flooring for kitchen tents that were being built, piles of high tech gear for lighting and sound, and stoves and pots and pans. Those last would be part of the noisy mock serenade made to the couple after their wedding. As Stavros was the person considered master of the rail station, a service for which he was paid an ample daily wage, he carried bills of lading and delivery notices, checked inventory and moved stock. He was a sort of sheriff balancing demands of the marketplace, and picking opportunities for himself. When he wasn't procuring goods and making his own business he was planning to meet up with Estafania. She had worked her way down the line. She was still active in her ambulance service further up the line. They exchanged a letter when they made a connection that made it to the sweetheart's location. The letters carried terms of endearment, perfumed powders, and eau de colognes.

Stevo Brakeman was having the time of his life as a delivery man for Stavros. This put him inside the wedding tent, inside the ladies tent, and inside what was now a cafeteria like dining hall. With so many different people, different tribes, nationalities, backgrounds, and hampers of different foods to deliver, the nutritious food was gorged by many, and the exchange of menu descriptions made a great variety, and diverse population. Each dish required a different root, pod, fruit, flower, leaf or stalk. It seemed every Bedoiun woman would make her own exotic dish. Then she would walk her bowl or tray through the dining hall offering samples. Stevo was there with new ingredients often, and tried everything, meeting everyone. He was constantly exposed to traditional customs, and looked upon as a talented asset. His timing seemed perfect whenever he arrived.

On the rail tracks Stavros was staging special rail cars for jubilant public officials, who had been invited to the wedding. Some had central air, bedrooms, and formal meeting rooms. After the wedding the officials, civil engineers, city planners, and managing personnel were going to oversee the building of the pharmaceutical research center.

This was the area of the city's blueprint that Ngongo and Alisa the showboat elephant were working, even as workers extended rail tracks, and added sidings. Additions to the track were being made in order to store building materials, in the first phase, mostly steel and concrete building materials. They were going to construct a concrete plant, and pour the foundations. Alisa's strength and coordination, affected by Ngongo with his toes stuck behind her ears made it easy work. They could pull or push rail cars loaded with materials into the exact storage location. Tahvo had been enlisted to make a diagram of all the materials arriving, he could read and write clearly, so he was going to be an important part of the operation, as a warehouse man. He was also designing a graphic plan of all the rail cars, and what each car held.

Tahvo was also being encouraged by Nevet, Steffie Toro's assistant, to apply for status as a voter. This would make it possible for him to be part of the referendums that could change the topmost point most natives knew in their lives at the railhead. Nevet was also looking at Tahvo as a possible Mr. Right. She thought they had friendship with potential. They were on the verge of becoming inseparable.

The bride's father hung around wherever he wanted. He took walks along the lake then took shipment of kids' sneakers with LED lights in the heels. He would find children helping their mothers, or hanging at the soccer field and make a big show of giving the right size of shoe to each child. He brought in a large fish tank, set it on blocks and filled it with junior-size goldfish. The kids loved this. He would step in when disputes arose in the wedding tent, or among the bride's attendants. He would count sequins on comparable gowns, and freshen everyone's tea being served constantly around the tent. He offered matchmaking advice to single ladies, and admired the figures of women who cried for attention. He talked with Touma Thomaz who admitted he loved Teriasandre y Ateriasandre. He befriended the bomb squad escapee who had filtered in with the crews bagging fertilizer in the lake's mud flats. He sent him back up the line in his private car because the bomb squad graduate insisted he was a qualified librarian. His next job was at the architectural study being organized as a tiny house next to Etienne Isti's home. The bride's father was very popular and mysterious, and never closed his eyes if he was greeted with a kiss, which was often. In truth he suffered from philemaphobia, the fear of kissing. In the men's shower he was dangerous with a wet towel. If he had wives or concubines he only spoke of the bride's mother. He told stories of a thousand, ancient Arab armies. He stayed on the lookout for men with blue eyes, and red hair as this was the sign of a vampire. Everywhere he saw supernatural beings and spirits, phantoms and accepted these visitations as entirely normal. He felt moments and people in the past or present always existed. Even suspended animation might lead to inescapable death, but you were still alive somewhere and always would be.

For all of these human characteristics he was ready to make a very expensive gift to his daughter. His largesse was a small favor. He knew she would leave his life and travel to the United States. He expected after she was married there would be descendants given to him by her. The exchange he considered an equal one. Each offering had the same status. He had a talent for whopping favors.

look into the skylight

THE GOOD OIL
is slang for truth

CHAPTER THIRTEEN

Tahvo, the native at the fountain who boarded the Jeep with Overview, and Nevet, Steffie Thom's assistant and parachute jump school partner, had become inseparable. After the second delay of the wedding ceremony the greatest happiness principle went into effect. Ateriasandre y Teriasandre, the prospective bride assured everyone that she would be able to recover from an extreme bout of food poisoning and she told her father that the correct action that provides the greatest happiness for most people is the best course. Ateriasandre was writing love notes to Touma Thomaz to reassure him that he was not responsible for this series of events. That story was a story just so tailored to fit the situation. It did result in a solution to a problem, and it did so efficiently. Even as sick as she was and having tremendous swings of confidence and fear.

Estaban Dae upon hearing that Ateriasandre was sick returned from the mountaintop gold mine leaving Cardinal and Sam to fend for themselves. He brought one of the two brother leaseholders from the mine, the male nurse and local doctor Stifen. As both Ateriasandre and Stifen spoke English with foreign emphasis in pronunciations, Ateriasandre began to take a fanciful and imaginative approach to her new medical angel. She began to recombine and invent his personality because of regional dialect and social group. Stifen is an original name for a man from Thailand. Stiifen is an original name for an Arabic man. The similarity began to make Stifen, a nurse and doctor from Thailand, the object of her underscored regional speaking manner. She was a Bedouin princess. He poured magical elixirs and cure-alls into her cup. She drew nearer to health then fell again into painful gasps. She was a beauty and her beauty was an obstacle to her elegance and gracefulness. In her health she did not lose but she did not win. He was a sensible knave. He was a snoot with another potion. He was honest except when he could take advantage or derive a benefit. If his Thai name, Stifen had not been so close to the Arabic Stiifen they would have conversed more effectively. Or, if he had been an Arabic Istifan, or an Istifanus. Her dialect and conversation emphasized a pointing up. Her illness was the thing that was not barely true. Neither understood the other well. It was if they each had no explanation for "Qanuipit." The Canadian Artic natives word for "How are you?"

When feeling well Ateriasandre y Teriasandre wrote letters emphasizing her love to Touma Thomaz. He was a zelophobic. That is someone who has a phobia for jealousy. He saw her illness as the result of random events. For Stifen, the would-be doctor, Touma felt nothing except the failure of expectations. He sarcastically announced to him, "I think you would have a better chance with her if you told her you were eighty years old.."

The love letters he received were extremely lovely but confused. One sounded as if it came from bottleneck theory. As if the words had gone onto the page after being narrowed through the neck of a bottle. There seemed to be parts of several conversations at the same time. This for example: "Please my eyeliner hues in the international news. Excuse me for the cake mix I'm waiting and my odd lot trading. Pardon me. Policy and politics I'm rating for matrix dot freighting." This note was hand delivered, signed and scented with her usual signature and perfume.

Another was hand delivered and praised January the thirty-first, the birthday of Touma Thomaz. In her letter she praised Touma and the date of his birth. Her recovery began after Ateriasandre's sister came to the hospital tent with a cure to restore her fitness. Stifen, the Thai nurse and doctor, thankfully began to draw an empty blank for ingredients and Ateriasandre's aunt insisted he stop his aggravating treatment. Ateriasandre's mother was still locked into a desert location and waiting for the wedding day in order to surprise her husband. She was staying at a distance in order to avoid coming into contact with Etienne Isti's *thurras,* those second wives. She wanted to present him with a *shen-nar*. The *chukkar* bird was plump, edible and delicious. Her husband would unwrap his *mendeel,* the head scarf wrapping at the sight of the gift of the delicious bird.

For Ateriasandre her mother had made a *baytheraan,* a bitter desert herbal remedy. This was presented to her by her oldest sister, who was *majnoon*, going crazy at the Thai doctor. Ateriasandre awoke out of a sound sleep, drank the alleviating solution and went back to sleep. Two hours later she awoke and stood beside her bed and spoke the word "Halimit." This word, which means "I dreamed," was news all around the camp. She was put back to bed and began to recover. When hearing of the news her mother said "Binit," the word for the feminine child.

As she began to recover Ateriasandre wrote a letter to Touma. She put on a *mudraga* and a headscarf and stood with the letter in hand outside the hospital doorway in the company of thirty-five people who were from the hospital, part of the wedding party, or there for the show.

Touma was called and presented with a love letter from Ateriasandre. The contents of the letter were private but the meeting of the two interrupted *shish-bish,* backgammon games, and began an upward journey of the soul. The camp began to think of the way things could be, rather than rely on the way things appeared to be. A myth was created which became an old wives' tale long after they met outside the doorway of the hospital. The awe-inspiring, mysterious and secret letter was a puzzle.

Touma, who was blinkered about Ateriasandre, read the letter in private and began an appreciation for Ateriasandre that lasted a lifetime. It contained a long quotation from a speaker in the British Parliament who rose from his seat on January 31, 1794. January 31 was Touma's birthday. The letter quoted the speaker on that day: "Illustrious man! Deriving honor less from the splendor of his situation than from the dignity of his mind. I cannot, indeed, help admiring the wisdom and fortune of this great man. By the phrase fortune I mean not in the slightest degree to derogate from his merit. But notwithstanding his extraordinary talents and exalted integrity, it must be considered as singularly fortunate that he should have experienced a lot which so seldom falls to the portion of humanity. For him it has been reserved to run the race of glory."

This letter made him feel surprise and pride. Ateriasandre was a student of American history and she was going to make things right. In the meantime her ommatophobia, the wariness of the evil eye, kept her on the lookout for foul spirits, and men who claimed to be more than mortal, and were nothing but a tempest in a teapot.

The great campsite seemed to double in size every day. After six days it was an enormous and great little city. Tahvo with Nevet by his side were marching from *shig* to *shig*, the area of each tent where visitors were welcome. Together they were making an original survey by mapping the distances between tents, and measuring and calculating the size of each structure. Nevet who was a Polynesian was going into each *marae*, each meeting place, with the greeting "Kia Ora!" Good health and good luck. In keeping company with Tahvo for the last few days she had begun to appreciate his charismatic personality. She admired him as an imaginable *tangata*.

While mapping the railyard and the new tent city, Tahvo was a *sheikh*, or a *consul*, or a *suzerain*, or the figurehead mayor. It was Nevet who was the trendsetter and despite the presence of good-for-nothing lotus eaters, and shiftless, work-shy boys, was able to find a way to enjoy the presence of everyone, and motivate each to a type of work that fit their ambition. Even the cricket playing boys including the wicketkeeper, the umpire, the bowler, the right-handed batsman and the night-watchman, helped her mastermind the encirclement of a bounty hunter who was prowling the grounds. After confiscating his manacles he was told to take his business elsewhere. Nevet's work ethic and ability to have specific goals and achievements with everyone made Tahvo imagine with her a life of connubial bliss. She could easily assess the presence of free riders and have them contributing.

As they visited every corner of the growing village they were joined by Tipene Stefaniya the U.N. representative who was in the village to organize a voting organization. He wanted to help a local electorate raise referendums. He was canvassing the area, writing and collecting names, and gathering information on possible resolutions. He fit in well with Tahvo and Nevet, in spite of their obvious closeness, and their flirtatious behavior. His walking from place to place with them became a source of amusement, and they entertained each other with assessments of everyone, from those that were helpless as a baby, the well-mannered, the working class, and the ill-mannered, the uncivilized and the impolite. They saw both gold diggers and scavengers. Everyone had a name and a camp address, and then unknowingly a tapestry of comment that was honest, funny and unique. Gossip and conjecture among the three was a source of great entertainment.

Every person the three met was told their future was on the ballot. They were given a quick rundown on what made them eligible to vote, and promised if eligible no one would be turned away. After Tahvo located their workplace, or their home on his regional map, Nevet would talk to them about employment skills, and experience. Lastly they were told, "If you do not vote we will be disappointed." Tipene made a note of their voting experience, and they moved on. Then the three began an amusing gabfest of gossip. Everyone's name was bandied about. The reason for this was Tipene was looking for chatter and the lowdown about Steffie Thom. No one yet knew she had changed her name to an aboriginal Steffie Toro. He was smitten by her. He was infatuated and swept off his feet. By gossiping he was hoping to learn more about her from Nevet, her administrative assistant. Despite his infatuation he tried to stay wily and artful in his gossip. There was a certain bandwagon effect about this. Each of the three by adopting a scuttlebutt tone began an increasing grapevine tattletale with the other two. The result was a sense of rumor. This began at lunch. Tipene knew that gossip was like cabbage. The best way to raise it was with a knife and fork.

They began by gossiping about a Bedouin lady seated near them at a table and playing whist. Tahvo referred to her as "as-Sitt-Fatima" a respectful name for a lady. They noticed she had filled her table with whist players. At whist she was very fortunate. Her play was not impulsive.

Everyone in the tent wanted to be acquainted with her. The *muzferr* hanging from the back of the chair had been filled many times by her as a midsummer midwife, an *accoucheuse*. She traveled the desert in the summer, but at her house in the mountains she showed a remarkable knowledge of European travel, and a good heart. She was thought to be an intimate of the mother of the bride, Ateriasandre. Among the most intimate. She had collected many players around her. They played whist for *cikara*, cigarettes, and *manga*, cans of mixed fruit nectar. Tahvo reported she was in the camp to watch over her most beautiful daughter.

As Nevet was near to finishing her lunch, the *inshallah*, the twenty year old son of the whist playing Fatima, came into the tent. After greeting his mother he was greeted and beckoned to the lunch table by Nevet. His name Ixtebe was well known. He had worked in the region at the gold mine, at the plastics factory, on the public waterworks project and at the train station. He was proficient at many tasks, and coming down from his mother's mountainside home, had lived in the Railhead during work projects since he was fifteen. He could read and spoke Arabic, English, French, and Spanish. His father, a Basque gentleman, had returned to Spain and not been seen for several years. The locals thought he had been killed fighting as a mercenary.

Ixtebe sat at the table with Nevet and Tahvo. Tipene began recruiting him to the bipartisan voting canvass that was based on moral considerations, and social and economic change. Tipene, who had a pleasant demeanor and extensive experience attracting capable candidates, wanted to take a straw poll from the other people in the tent to see if Ixtebe had what it takes to become a genuine public servant. Tipene wanted to see if Ixtebe would join the voting drive aimed at stabilizing and healing the region and become a member of their coalition. He wondered if the young gentleman would be simon-pure. So Tipene began to talk about voting rights in accordance with the facts.

After a quick rundown assuring Ixtebe, "Your vote will count," he cautioned him that mistakes are caused within the electorate by lack of attention. The tribalized region needed to retain experienced public servants. At the polling places no eligible voters would be turned away. One vote in a small region could decide the election.

Ixtebe who was polite and quiet in the face of the excited Tipene said little. Once when Tipene asked him if he was married, he responded, "I am too poor to marry any woman without some fortune, and too proud to marry any woman without one." This brought laughter to the room as Tipene had managed to get the attention of everyone in the room with his voting enrollment speech. Tipene's attempt at political backscratching with Ixtebe had gotten the attention of Fatima, his mother. When Tipene asked Ixtebe if he was married, Fatima sat straight up, and looked over the room, as she too giggled at his answer. Her thoughts focused on a customary coupling which made common sense.

Tahvo and Nevet nodded in agreement after Ixtebe rose from his chair to stand close to his mother, and spoke quietly with her. Both

Tahvo and Nevet raised their arms when Tipene asked for a show of hands calling the young man a "possible candidate and line of action." Tipene then began a census of the entire room by a show of hands. Just then the cricket team entered the room and called upon Ixtebe to join them in their game. He said, "Si," and the cricket team glad handed him out the doorway. This display of brotherhood by the cricket team showed his popularity was not counterfeit, fake or bogus in any way. Politics and voting rights enrollment in the tent continued, as war without bloodshed was played out. As if it were a Chinese room and it is a man who has real thoughts not a computer.

The end of the accepted break time for lunch came to an end, and the run of the mill crowd left, opening up seats for the garden variety everybody and his brother, gathering. The rush into the tent followed a noisy, engine whistle from the latest product laden train arriving at the station. There was a rush into the tent of a wood gathering troupe fresh from the train. Electricity running along new poles being set by workmen meant that burning wood was not the only source for heat and light. Still, there seemed to be a number of people who would like to put in a stock of wood, which when doused with kerosene made a charged up crowd gather at night.

Among the wood gathers who stood outside were some Russian ladies. First one, then two, then three came into the tent. They gathered in an open space in the center. First one began to dance. They all spoke with heavy accents but some knew a few English phrases, the language that was the dominant local tongue in camp. The first Russian lady to dance announced loudly, "I work hard. I play hard, too." She began what looked like a waggle dance. She would move in a straight line, waggling her abdomen, then turn clockwise, or counterclockwise, dancing to her fellow honeybees. The bee's dancing choreography speaks to the other members of her hive.

Tipene who was sitting with Nevet and Tahvo tried small talk. Speaking quietly he said, "In my opinion she is too large for a beauty."

Nevet and Tahvo looked to each other, and remarked on what they thought was a good sense of humor. Then Nevet offered, "I think she has blue eyes, and a clear complexion."

Tahvo shook his head in agreement, and offered, "Graceful."

The dancer continued her bee dance. The honeybee's dance maps out directions to a food source, or a new nesting site. Nevet then began a string of commentaries toward the growing line of Russian ladies.

Soon the center of the tent was filled with ladies from Odessa, Kiev, Saint Petersburg, Moscow, Siberia and the Ural Mountains. Eleven ladies in all, a banker's dozen, and finally Ektarina Tomi, the mother of Stevo Brakeman the Russian encryptologist who had been handing over information on the war, and the rebuilding of the village. As the Railhead's station agent he had seen his mother and her touring Russian debutantes arrive. Instead of bringing men on sightseeing tours to Russia, Ektarina was bringing the curious and adventurous risk takers to more than an armchair adventure. She hoped within the wilderness region to find a comfortable atmosphere for the ladies to find romance with men. And find men with good intentions. They were also Ektarina's posse, as she hoped to bring her son home and away from his double agent service. She was on a sightseeing tour with her harem. She promised the girls unlimited introductions. At the moment things were playing out well and the lunch tent gave them plenty of room to mingle. If you were introduced to one, you could meet another, and then meet more ladies. Things were on the up and up.

Stevo Brakeman, the son of Ektarina Tomi had kept from view when he saw his mother arrive at the station. He had written her by way of untraceable letter through a dispatch mailing service. She had not been a doting mother. He thought he should send her as many rubles as he could afford and the peace of mind that came with knowing your underachieving child was in good health and happy. He hoped this would smooth over her worries about the little nipper. He was forthcoming in his letter, and underestimated the bond she felt with him. Like an angry bear she had come all this way to find him. Primarily to defuse his dangerous employment. He was a spy. The outcome could have consequences. She wanted him off his ride before he rode the pale horse.

Nevet looked over the roomful of Russian courtliness, and grinned at Tahvo and Tipene.

Tipene had been asking a few questions about Steffie Toro, and wedding dresses, then how the ceremony of the wedding would play out. Tipene and Nevet discussed traditional Western wedding dresses, and then some non-traditional wedding dresses.

"Some wedding dresses, all white, make the bride look like a cream puff," said Tipene.

"Oh, look at her," said Nevet to Tahvo. "She is so delicate and modest. That's her sister, the other one. She has the oddest figure my eyes have ever beheld."

Tahvo was very much into the gossipy way of talking at the moment. Plus, his background in reading famous literature led to his comment. "Her, she, Miss Siberia. She is the belle of the family. And her, at the card table. She is a fine girl, a sweet countenance and an agreeable smile."

Nevet turned her head and flashed a huge grin at Tahvo's observation, and raised her foot to his under their table. Tahvo didn't turn but started to speak but not before Tipene interjected something from the back of his mind.

"The wedding dresses I've seen are poufy. Do you know what I mean? Like a lamp shade over your shoulders, and some tissue paper. They are sort of like a cocoon, and bushy. I guess that's sort of a free spirit."

Nevet spoke again. "Look at her. At the whist table. She is rather tall and large. She is very elegant."

The elegant Russian lady standing at the whist table had put everyone there at ease. She was entertaining a large circle of both sexes. She had been chatting since she had arrived, and her voice had a musical tone to it. She was witty and amusing in discussing the social life of Russia. She was angry, she said, to have to leave her papa but was hoping to find a superior life, one that would contrast with the one she was being offered in her own country.

Tipene, who had been frustrated in his attempt to find a chance to open a revealing discussion about Steffie Toro, was holding back an impulsive question. Was she going to the wedding, and did she need an escort? A date? Would she go on a date to the wedding with Tipene? In his frustration and anger with himself for being so bashful about asking Nevet about Steffie, he began to make awkward comments. He hoped lubberly talk would up the level of surprise in their gossip. So he said about a young Russian lady who was bouncing around the room taking pictures, and chatting, "She is just chatting about her cap, or her hair ribbons, or her corset, or her toga for all we know."

Nevet laughed at this, and Tipene added the question, "Have you seen Steffie Toro? I saw her the other day. I thought she had on a toga."

Tahvo and Nevet both laughed at this, then Tipene asked, "Do you think she will go to the wedding? Will she be at the wedding?"

Nevet started to answer, "Steffie is going to go with…" Here she stopped, and at the far end of the tent Ektarina Tomi, Stevo Brakeman's mother made a noisy entrance into the tent and stood on a small stage with the entire cricket team. She had gathered all the young men from the cricket contest and brought them into the tent so that everyone would be able to enjoy a very public introduction to the entire group of Russian ladies. Extebe was on his way to the train station to bring Stevo Brakeman back to the tent. Stevo had loaded their luggage into the *kibitka*, the railroad's cart. Ixtebe insisted that Stevo be at the public introduction of the Russian ladies because he spoke a little Russian, and should see this.

Ixtebe asked, urged, and insisted that Stevo bring himself and the luggage to the lunch tent. Stevo spoke politely, *gospodin*, but

Ixtebe would not take no for an answer. Stevo had a few *kopek*, but could not buy off the muscular, much larger young boy. Ixtebe was friendly, persistent and enthusiastic about returning to the tent. His dutiful and gung ho attitude to be the hero to the Russian ladies by returning with their luggage, made Stevo a fan of his avid persistence. So he decided to approach the delivery like a constructive daydream and make a prominent hero of himself, too. So Ixtebe and Stevo joined together on the job with gusto, and grabbed the cart. Quickly they hand pulled it to the back entrance of the lunch tent, next to the stage. Then with a competitive exuberance, and a wave to the stage filled with ladies singing a simple song about sons and daughters, both walked into the tent and took seats in the front row. Stevo's mother, Ektarina Tomi, stood to the side of the singing girls and looked sophisticated and charming. Stevo and his mother made eye contact and each held others attention through the end of the girl's song.

After the song ended, with much laughter and cheering, and holding a bouquet of flowers out to the girls, she turned her back to the audience and said to the girls, "Breathe. Smile. And you will stand out." Then she turned to the still cheering crowd and began a sales pitch that embarrassed a few, but had men with lederhosen, horseback riders in jodhpurs, bike riders in pedal pushers, soccer players in sweat pants, motorcycle riders in stovepipe pants, a Pakistani in shalwars, a dancer in toreador pants, an army private in fatigues, and an Oxford type wearing baggy pants and a *diamante,* jewelry made from paste to glitter like diamonds, all generate reactions that held a syrupy sentimentality. To begin she raised her hand and yelled above the crowd, "Don't fall in love the first day." Then she began individual introductions and descriptions that brought laughter, more from the girls than the crowd of men.

She would have each girl step forward, be introduced, then add a descriptive phrase such as "Honest, loyal, intelligent." Or "Energetic, merry, well-balanced." About all the girls she said, "The ladies have spent hours in preparation, and are here to put their best foot forward." Some could kick the *kazatka*, the Russian dance. Others would cha-cha, or samba. Then she explained everyone was invited to write a letter to anyone who had been introduced onstage. She explained, "Use the word hello, not dear. Send a photo. Don't brag about wealth. Don't use the word love in the first letter."

Throughout this entertainment she and her son kept a close eye on one another, and were overjoyed at the sight of the other. Yet, each was a spy. She a Mata Hari, and he a decoy good at intelligence gathering. They were enjoying each other's company, but were speechless. They could not yet speak to one another.

In the back of the room Nevet, Tahvo and Tipene had stayed for the whole show. They laughed, guffawed and giggled constantly. Each thought they were in a coliseum seeing a show so large it made them lean toward the stage to get a good look. They could not stop laughing. They wisecracked that this one was a contortionist, and that one a ventriloquist. The history of each girl on the stage was revealed to them in a brightly lit show. They appreciated it.

At the show's end Ixtebe, who had sat in the front row, rushed to the opening in the tent and began lining up suitcases in front of the stage. All the girls spoke to him like a long lost friend, and he was joined by remaining members of the cricket squad hoping to impress the girls. They were impressed.

Stevo Brakeman stepped to the downstage edge of the riser, and spoke up to his mother. "What you said made me think of..."

That was all Ixtebe heard. He was busy complimenting the girls.

In the back of the tent that had housed the performance without a marquee, Tipene turned to Nevet and said, "Did you say Steffie was going to the wedding? With who?"

Nevet turned to him and answered, "She had a date, but he's not going to be here. Captain Oliver Overview. I should tell you this. He's going on a mission, and won't be around. You might ask her."

Tipene had finally gotten the information he was after.

on the train, on the trestle

Cubicle Monkey

A cubicle monkey is the IT specialist.

CHAPTER FOURTEEN

Captain Oliver Overview was planning an extracurricular activity. He was going to have to do it with the aid and knowledge of Brigadier General Stevy Thomasine. It was supposed to be secret. The General compared the mission to a Pony Express run. One Army Captain, and two Russian journalists on a plane to the United States for a debriefing of the two journalists.

The debriefing process meant they would be in separate rooms possibly with a connecting plate glass window. They would be well fed and well treated. But they would stay in these rooms with a cot and a table, until they had satisfied the questioners. They would be questioned like they were returning from a mission. They would be faced with difficult questions. They could be questioned intensely. Then they would be cross-examined by other questioners. There might be quarrels or squabbles. There might be differences in answers and then reconciliations. They would hope for honest brokers and go-betweens who would try to intercede. They would try not to be involved in scandals. They could offer quick cooperation. Or, they could make rash and impulsive choices. They could give gruff replies and dangerously try to escape. Or, the questioners could be half-hearted in their care. Neither of the two journalists wanted to be forced to identify what was missing in their picture window. They would have to hope for sunshine at the end of their rainbow.

The General was a student of history, and a student of mythological episodes. He was a student of the war waged by mythological creatures. Some creatures waged war on the race of men. The Sphinx slaughtered men who could not solve its riddle. The Cyclops held men of Odysseus captive. There were basilisks that could kill by their breath, or even a look. Triton was a fish and a man. His control of ocean waves meant he could drown an entire city. Midas could turn anything into gold, stirring men to war with other men. Within her misery box, Pandora held all that men would shadow box, if it were loosed. The General told Overview if a plan to fly to the USA was-without his help, it would be like forever pushing a stone uphill. Like Sisyphus.

The General had problems of his own touching on secrecy. Information from the source known as Shetland pony had alerted an outside intelligence source on the status of the battlefield, and the presence of U.N. forces at the Railhead. The source had informed on the re-building status of the region and been able to pinpoint information being reported by the intelligence unit of General Thomasine. Everyone monitored what everyone else knew, and the General knew that others knew what the General, and his staff knew. There was a leak. It could be an individual, a reporting station, a code break at a receiving station, or it could be a managed individual at a headquarters location. Everyone was nervous. The phobia for foreign languages is xenoglossaphobia. The phobia for hell is hadephobia. Atelophobia is imperfection.

The General compared Overview's mission to a Pony Express run. They had a couple of Russian "belles letteres" they could fly from the region because they were willing to go. That would eliminate one possible source. The two journalists were part of a London News Bureau. Going to the U.S. appealed to the Russians. Overview was encouraging the General to debrief the two stateside. The General wanted to send them to Las Vegas, into an air base. Who wouldn't want to go to Las Vegas? There is a Russian population there. If the two were spies maybe they would trip themselves up.

Comparing the flight mission to a Pony Express ride was testimonial to the General as a hard-working student of American history. The twice a week runs of the Pony Express beginning in 1860 ran a parallel route to Highway U.S. 50 through Nevada. The General on leave had taken a ride through the region a few years after the commemorative 100th year of the Pony Express. The original trail has long been obliterated by time. When faced by young recruits for a disciplinary action after drinking, or fighting, the General regularly informed recruits they would fail the loyalty oath of the Pony Express. Then he offered recruits facing charges the opportunity of a simple explanation. Simple explanations are better than complex ones.

Overview intended to help the General change his mind. He wanted the two Russians recruited to his plan to meet and intimidate the harassing phone callers who'd created a sad and sorry situation for his sister, and his niece. He wanted the Russian journalists on the spot with a camera rolling, and a pen in hand. Recruiting the General to his plan wasn't the best way of harnessing the two journalists into mission oriented training. The General would come up with smoke out questions. What would happen if? Or, a question like "Was Buffalo Bill Cody a Pony Express rider?" "Oh Aye, *he was again he was not*."

Overview had to generate a plan that would be one for the books. To begin this he shaped for himself a disguise. For the past seven days he had been growing a moustache. Military standards state that hair must be tapered at the back of the neck. If you do not have a moustache at the start of the course, you may not start one during the course. His moustache made him look like a Wild West villain. He would continue to let it grow until it would wave in the blustery wind. He also decided to become a very likeable, easy going guy whose moroseness had becalmed. He had outlasted a few American

Presidents in government service. He hoped to outlast at least a couple more in giving aid to fellow servicemen and veterans by supplying them with macaronic verse. He needed a change.

After burning the midnight oil to complete his plan, on a pretense he approached the two Russians, Chefo and Kiwini both experienced Russian journalists, working out of London. He began to talk about the opportunities for them in the United States if they could only get a ride there. On a temporary visa, or a green card they could work and play. With the right connections they could find a way to make the move permanent. He talked about the economic stability of rural Nevada. “The booming towns of Las Vegas and Reno may have ups and downs,” he said, “but the agriculture, mining, and on hand tourism in the state in small towns has staying power.” Both Chefo and Kiwini were perplexed by this. The Russian phrase for perplexed persons is *ozadachennyy chelovek*. The word for boogeyman is *bugimen*. They had already given an enthusiastic “Yes” to General Stevy Thomasine for a trip to Las Vegas, and given a complete report on their journalism reporting at the Railhead. They had stood in front of a camera with the growing tent city in the background. They had reported on the drifting armies in the desert. They had played a simple role.

Overview told them gold mines were located in fifteen counties in Nevada. If there were tough economic times the price of gold usually went up. Mining for gold is a pillar of strength in Nevada. Traveling the state was never a problem. Cars and trucks were constantly bought and sold in Nevada. There were ground breaking ceremonies for construction projects almost every day somewhere in the state. There were drillers and engineers who could be a constant source of news. If you wanted to be a student, the state had accelerated education programs. You could study wherever you wanted to. With their skills and credentials they could take an apartment in Montreal, and study from there.

The two journalists had to blink back tears. The idea of contentment in Nevada seemed real but they were losing confidence in Overview. Nonetheless their *plat du jour*, their dish of the day, was a *mot just*. Their agreement was to get on the plane and out of action. If the joke was on them they were going to enjoy it.

The two journalists were counting the days, the halcyon days of fine weather, tranquility and prosperity the trip to Las Vegas promised. In 1700 Peter the Great after adopting the Julian calendar made January 1 the beginning of the New Year. Lenin adopted the Gregorian calendar in 1918, after the Revolution. The Julian calendar was thirteen days behind the Gregorian calendar. The country changed on January 31 and the next day was February 13. Russia also tried an Eternal calendar from 1929 to 1940. Each week had six days and each month lasted thirty days.

A change in their day jobs was coming for the two Russian journalists. Within a month an Achilles heel from *prisiadka* choreography would be overcome by the marching sequence of the country dance, and they would promenade their partners in the style of western square dances. The two Russians would learn to *dos si do*.

The General went to the tent city at the Railhead to have a look around. The place was becoming the amusement park of Etienne Isti, the father of the bride. Wedding plans had been renewed after her return to good health. An engineering firm was outlining their plans, and staking off areas for their new research center. The General was forced to recant his denunciation of the influx of so many differing peoples. The bustling enterprise was the beginning of commerce. Men of business were able to give him short and comprehensive reports. In tents near the lunch tents there were pool tables and bowling. There were many recreations that were manful not sinful.

The General joined a tall, beautiful, blond Russian woman by the lakeside who was hitting golf balls. She was wearing a poncho, and pulled a couple of golf balls from under it.

The General couldn't understand her at first when she asked, "You palay arund?"

After he understood, he laughed and said, "Yes, I want to play a round."

He began a speech to her with his usual pleasant demeanor on the future of the ballot. She gave him a quick rundown on how to waggle and address the ball with your hands relaxed.

At the compound the Russians had taken the final step in materializing as informers by removing blindfolds they had worn while seated in the one vehicle convoy Overview led to the classified location. A little used airstrip nearby, a dirt road widened by an occasional hedgehopping plane, was the target for a cargo plane deadheading into the airstrip. Overview set up a card table in the middle of the grassy center, and served them a plate of *zuppa inglese*, the Italian desert cake made with rum and candied fruits. Steffie Thom had shipped the cake in and made presents of it to everyone.

The Captain had grown sarcastic, and said, "Yeah, sure, this is the transit lounge," and the two Russians sat at the table and ate the cake, with cool water.

The plane had flown off course, and was behind schedule, so Overview walked around the edges of the compound looking at the vehicles, trailers and a motorcycle that had begun to look like an abandoned junkyard. He came to an RV size camper that was part of the original communications outpost. All the gear had been stripped out of it when more comfortable and sizeable trailers had been shipped aboard cargo planes. The little tin can had four flat tires, and the battery was missing. Overview could not have cared less if replacement parts would give him the same camper, so he pulled a battery from a Jeep and put it in the camper.

After he took off the air filter it started. Then he looked over at Chefo the Russian and yelled, "Hey, the highlight of your career might be losing the race to Las Vegas. Or, the highlight of your career might be winning the race to Las Vegas."

Chefo was a sizable man, and could have been a bouncer if not a journalist, came over and began taking wheels and tires from other vehicles and replaced the flattened ones on the RV.

When Chefo had trouble with the tire wrench Overview said, “You look like the orchestra type.”

When it was running and had four tires Overview began a running dialogue with Chefo. When he sat behind the wheel, and Overview directed him to bang the bumper against the vehicle behind to clear space for the vehicle to pull out, with Chefo at the wheel, the engine died.

Overview said, “Maybe you would be better at selling encyclopedias door to door.”

When the RV, a silver looking tin can finally cleared the area of the junkyard, Overview pounded him on the back and said, “You drive this thing like a Missouri mule.”

By the time the air cargo plane flew over the compound notifying them of its arrival, they had cleared a trail so they could take a shortcut to the airstrip. Once on board the plane it wasn’t standing room only. The RV raced over the rough grass track with Overview at the wheel, and was tied down in its paddock aboard the aircraft. The pilot was from Florida. When he was in his home state the pilot liked to hydroplane a motorboat. He never cut his engine motors. He and Overview had been sentries during boot camp. After the pilot executed a takeoff, he flew a tight bend and throttled down to keep the seams together. The two Russians were aboard and handed documents, then signed statements giving them temporary visas. They flew away into the darkening sky trailing a moving spot of red light from the plane’s tail.

The light behind was a ghost image leaving a trail for wild animals, natives, isolated deserters, and young, attractive, verbal, intelligent, successful people. YAVIS, noticed the noisy plane while the sun was setting on the horizon. YAVIS. Those are young, attractive, verbal, intelligent, successful people. Steffie Thom was one who noticed the plane on the horizon. Nevet was one who saw it approaching the mountain top, gold mining property. Ateriasandre saw it. Touma Thomaz saw it, and so did Tipene Stefaniya, the UN representative. Sam saw it too, standing with Sutepano, the Thailand mining engineer outside the elevator shaft that led to the lower levels of the gold mine.

The plane's pilot hadn't turned off his engine after landing or, before takeoff, in the middle of barren, rough ground, on the little used road. The plane with people aboard might attract animals, natives or isolated deserters. A rhino might stumble down the road. Monkeys, baboons, or even wildebeest might be attracted to whatever smells came from the plane. Even the smell of diesel fuel. When the pilot gunned the engine and adjusted for the cargo load he lifted off and headed for the nearest high point to orient his navigator/copilot. The wind was stiff so he flew slightly into the crosswind, crabbing, to offset the drift. At the top of his climb he banked the plane into a circle above the mountaintop and waited for the navigator to correct their heading.

In a seat by a window in the cargo area Overview sat belted to his chair. Everyone and everything was belted down. Overview looked out the window at the mountaintop mine. He thought of the rumors circulating about the precious metal that could be found there. The grapevine talk and the gossip. No one had ever been able to put an end to the persistent rumors. From his leather satchel he pulled a fistful of papers ordered destroyed as part of the change to a new crew at the intelligence gathering compound. There were letters of credence, deeds, and affidavits. Customary protocol was to cut the documents to ribbons and discard them. With a loud grunt, and showy wave he stood with the papers in hand, then flushed them out the windy gust of the window with a wave. The papers scattered in the slipstream behind the airship, and floated toward the ground, blowing in a scattershot across the mountaintop. A pair of eagles stooped from their nest on a cliff, swooping down to snatch at the collection of papers, the dossiers filled with information but twisting like confetti in the wind. The aquiline birds flew back to their high nesting place when the stuff turned out to be something they could not easily devour. They perched in their aerie and searched for other spoils below.

In front of the entrance to the mine Sam and Sutepano were being held at gunpoint. Cardinal Octillion had read all the signs left behind. They were carved into rocks and rock faces, carved onto the side of concrete structures, and written on the walls of the gold mine. Natives and native workers left behind sign of their own creativity. Two dotted circles and an arrow on the side of a hard rock cliff pointed to the radio shack. A rectangle with an arrow pointed to the water tank containing drinkable water. Below the eagle aerie but above the depression where the mine opened was a half-circle and three lines pointing skyward. This was the sign of the *southern lights*. The southern hemisphere has a nighttime light show caused by solar winds. The *aurora australis*. The sign of the planet Neptune was carved on the outside of one of the bunkhouse cabins. The mystical planet is denoted by a large U and a sword through it from below. Neptune is supposed ruler over "plants used for the purpose of intoxication." This sign he found at a distance further up the mountain.

With Estaban Dae, and Stifen, Sutepano's brother and the male nurse and doctor, both below and enjoying the festivities surrounding the wedding, Cardinal had spent some time thinking about the recompense, the repayment, he would resign himself to accept. His idea was to rob Sutepano's mine and let the mine owners take it in stride, and make the best of it. The three, Sam, Cardinal and Sutepano were finally alone after the work force couldn't be prevented from scampering to the feasting and wedding ceremony that could be seen every night by the light of huge bonfires, and arc lights, set up near the rail tracks to guide trains into the station. The men at the mine had stayed on their palace of nature, each for their own reason.

Sutepano could speak English, Thai, and Spanish. Cardinal could speak English, Swahili and related native languages, and fluent Spanish. Sam could speak English and very little Spanish. Cardinal was more worried about Sam putting up a fight than he was worried about resistance from Sutepano. So he spoke only Spanish, and Sutepano had to interpret the instructions, and orders Cardinal gave in a commanding voice. Cardinal ordered Sutepano to interpret everything he said.

A situation began in the early morning in the bunkhouse when Cardinal and Sutepano entered the doorway. Sam was standing at the table putting apples, biscuits, and cucumbers in a paper sack lunch, los juanillos. Sutepano was standing in front of Cardinal with his arms raised.

Cardinal said to Sutepano, "Camine para atras hacia mi voz." He poked a nickel plated pistol in the back of Sutepano, who said to Sam, "Walk backward toward my voice."

Sam could see the situation and recognized the look of fear on Sutepano, and the look of anger on Cardinal.

As he walked with his back toward the two men, Cardinal said, "Tiene armas?"

Sutepano said, "Do you have any weapons?"

Sam held up the paper sack and dropped it to the floor.

Cardinal shouted, "Extienda los brazos a los lados."

Sutepano said to Cardinal, "Calmese," "calm down," and then said to Sam, "Put your hands out to your sides."

Cardinal said to Sutepano, "No me chinques," "don't cheat me," then said, "Manos atras."

Sutepano said to Sam, "Hands behind you."

Sam was careful to do as he was told, but blurted out one of the few Spanish phrases he was familiar with. "Con que le pogo?"

Sutepano was surprised by Sam's question, but Cardinal leaned forward pushing the pistol into his back, and laughed as he said, "What did he hit you with?"

Both Sutepano and Cardinal said in near unison, Sutepano following Cardinal's voice, "Cuando fue eso?" "When was that?"

That ended conversation and Sutepano and Sam were told to stand in front of the bunkhouse door with their backs to one another, handcuffed by each hand to the other. Then they were waved out the door, walking back to back, with Cardinal giving directions, "a la izquierda," to the left, and "a la derecho," to the right. "No se muera," he said. Do not move. "Sientese." Sit down.

This episode had started at dawn when Sutepano found Cardinal in the principal building's office. He had smashed the display cases containing sample ore, nuggets and refined gold bars. These had been on display for years, and kept in the locked cases.

Cardinal's response to Sutepano's barking voice, "Tenga cuidado," "be careful," was "Cuanto cuesta cada cosa." How much is each item worth?

When Sutepano said, "Salga de aqui," "leave here," Cardinal said, "Vio a alguien cerca?" Did you see anyone nearby?

After this interaction and the capture of Sam, Cardinal began calling Sutepano, "el mero mero." The main man. Un apodo, a nickname that even a botella, a bottle would never completely allow Sutepano to forget.

After robbing the office Cardinal wanted to go into the gold mine one last time to chip high grade ore from spots left for assayers, visitors and tourists to view. To do it he had to handcuff Sam to the elevator support cable. It passed through the other side of the handcuffs as he lowered Cardinal and Sutepano into the depths of the mine. He turned off the engine, apague el motor, to listen for a gunshot after he had lowered the men into the mine. He stood in the rain waiting for an hour then through the intercom was told, "Mire hacia arriba." Look up. He could hear both men laugh below, so he raised them on the elevator.

Cardinal asked him when he was releasing him from the handcuff, "Hay testigos?" Are there witnesses?

Sam responded, "Llovia?" Was it raining?

On the top, at the elevator landing. Cardinal in the darkness shouldered his heavy burden of weapons, and gold and said one last time to Sutepano, "Dorado. El mero."

Sutepano said to Cardinal, "No regrese aqui." Do not come back here. Then he said to Sam, "No regrese." Do not return. Then he walked away from both men toward his office.

the lady in the light as fireflies light

Tabby

That tabby wears ambition, and chews shamrocks,
sleeps in morning glories.

CHAPTER FIFTEEN

The wedding preparations at the Railhead were a providence that would enlighten everyone.

They created an uplifting lesson of fortune, and invented a new thunderbolt for getting to the bottom of fatherhood. Very few compromises were made, yet everyone got what they wanted. The bride's oldest sister loudly commanded she was in charge of the wedding, and all its preparations. She did so in a voice assembling everyone that shared a taxi, a train, a camel, a motor coach, or a horse carriage to the region of the Railhead. There was constant hand shaking and head kissing to go along with congratulations among everyone. The inside story most frequently told was the magnificent affair, and the heavenly vicinity had created a deux ex machina. The surprising development had made the area of the wedding tent city an arcade. Under the roof of the arcade, supported by baffling formations, and relieving arches, even wizened people, the old, the dowager, the snowy-haired, the senile and doddering, would be healthy, active, and vigorous. Sprightly and spry. Rhytiphobia, fear of wrinkles, could be forgotten. This gave rise to dancing and dinner parties, and fun and gaiety. Opinions contrary to your own began to be welcome. This was the inside story in an open space where there was public speaking on inertia, the tendency of a body to remain at rest, and dynamics, unseen forces that altered the motion of bodies. Illness, injury, loneliness and madness declined. The bride's sister was pulling strings to satisfy appetites of every kind.

The bride's father had helped achieve this, all the while thinking of his distant soulmate, the bride's mother who stayed at a distance in the desert delivering messages daily to her daughter, and sending small gifts to her husband. He built his own private rail car into a mobile palace which extended on its own track to the center of the tent city. He imagined this a love nest where he would reunite with his first wife in an erotic frenzy, and they would stay together on their own, in their secret apartment.

Though he had a fear of lightning, he stood in a fierce and stormy wind one night outside his palace station. He wondered, why do people share with nature the thoughts that unlock their delusions of grandeur, or their primitive nature, or the recognition that they have lost their center of gravity? Why do men tell others of their wild or fabricated illness? Why do men go berserk, as if they are in a frenzy, and act like they are married to nature, folie a deux? When the storm passed Etienne Isti's dementia passed and his thoughts returned to women in his life that inspired his passion. Both his wife, and his daughters.

He was a man very much under his own control, but lightning made him feel unhinged. He was all there. Sober, sensible and reasonable.

Around him he had supported the peculiar notions of his daughters. Because of the delays in the wedding date, first because of the bride's illness, and then because of the desire to accommodate the huge cluster that crowded and jostled like a coterie, the date was firmly set by the bride and groom. Ateriasandre y Teriasandre after recovering from her illness had begun to go into orbit around the groom, Touma Thomaz. He read it as an aftermath of her illness. This yielded from him the same dedication from him to her. Both wore the mufti of their concentric circles and professed each was judiciously courting the other. Ateriasandre openly enjoyed being courted by her future husband. Touma told her he searched every day in his heart, and in the real world, an ideal marriage environment for his future wife.

All the while children swirled in noisy groups around the tent city making ready for the wedding. Around the edges of the city, goats were nibbling at everything. The untended young billies and nannies were owned by Bedouin tribesmen, and off the menu. Most of the gathered Bedoo were indulging in cafeteria style meals of exotic cuisine. The bride's father surrounded himself with new visitors and smoked sweetened, cavendish cakes of tobacco. To his new friends this was an exotic change from his usual strong, dark tobacco such as latakial. Titles of respect, and legends on coat of arms were obliging conversations made with raised voices. To mingle those conversations with the ordinary, Etienne gave handy hints on home decorating, and discussed reasonably priced, oriental carpets.

The bride's elder sister, and Etienne's daughter was relying on the gossip that surrounded her to bring to everyone a dose of happiness. She created a collection of ladies suites and efficiency rooms which could be turned into dormitories, rumpus rooms, or boudoir for sitting, or dressing. Some were sky blue, some were pink, and all were perfumed. Silk cloth hung from the walls, and lace decorated the furniture. There were separation panels for privacy, china for serving tea, vases to collect the peduncle stems of flowers, cushions for Bedouin accustomed to sitting on the earth, and clocks so that everyone was on the same interval and mainspring. There were seasonal clothes for everyone.

The Brigadier General Stevy Thomasine was entertained by the orchestral parts of the tangled, energetic gathering. He watched it all constantly, bag and baggage. He didn't see how anyone could hold the reins on all the melodies, the rhythms, and the noisemakers. At the same time he recognized a giddy, unyielding collection of unwritten rules. Giddy because it made you lightheaded to make fun of them and afterwards recognize they were an enormous contribution to appropriate behavior. It took composure and talent to obey the gigantic gimmick of respectability. In the tent city it was better to be well behaved.

The General steered himself toward common sense examination of unchecked and unruly outlaws. Every man, woman and child would give an explanation, and a motive for their presence in the tent city, and the Railhead. Some had hidden agendas. None were sent packing for being unmasked as a vagabond, or being outright refugees. Bounty hunters were told to find the cooling fires of creation and expelled from the camp. After they were sent to out-of-the-way observation posts, everyone who was out of the ordinary, or exotic, or wild, tried to outperform, outshine, and leave other tent city campers swirling in their wake. The backcountry neighbor with a rundown plan to book midnight junkets to see comets, or the milky way and outfit naturalists with equipment and duds, would outdo the adventurer who offered a small orchestra to accompany a plump lady who would sing from a vista view where the horizon would include the probability of hush-hush gold knuckles of rock. There were scalawags and troublemakers who would scan the new arrivals and skim their purse.

The General noticed some were pretending to be scofflaws, others were real lawbreakers who did not have a cashier with enough currency to make their own company jacket. Everyone was chasing the well-to-do and their loot. There seemed to be some on easy street. Other types formed lines behind them. The General observed the lesson that an offer laid at one's feet should be taken out of the closet. He noticed some were pretending to be rolling in dough, but that was a chink in their armor. Those could be penniless.

After the General introduced himself to the Russian lady golfer, he also introduced himself to her chaperone and escort, Ektarina Tomi, the mother of the Russian spy, Stevo Brakeman. When the General mentioned by name the lady golfer, Ektarina said, "Don't fall in love with a name." Ektarina knew that the best companion for the General might be one that was young but not immeasurably young. The General was not wet behind the ears, but his instantaneous attraction to his golfer girlfriend had given him boundless energy. It would be imprudent and inconsistent with the character of the General to be attracted to a girl with whom he was incompatible. It would also be a confusing entanglement if she gave her heart to someone else. Ektarina decided to throw light on the pair and see if this was a figment of their imagination. When she did fathom their attraction to one another the impression she got was like a castle in Spain. An affair between the two looked like it could be squeaky clean. They were both juvenile enough for mental gymnastics. The General's creativity with the girl made him feel like he had landed on his feet.

Ektarina's son, Stevo Brakeman had been reacting to the presence of his mother and General Thomasine with prompt and swift reaction. He was always ready to do any business that arrived by train at the Railhead. Stevo's mother was used to being in the driver's seat, and saw the situation of her son as a spy as appalling. She was here at the Railhead to weaken his hold on his position. A position he could prosper without. He used the words go-between to her, but to her he was still a tiny, small, pint-sized baby. She wanted her wholesome son defanged and pulled from his keyhole observations. She studied his physiology and wanted his loyalty to begin with himself. She mocked him by inquiring if he need a criminal accomplice. She was a chaperone, not a convoy for troops. This idea of herself as a co-conspirator, or accomplice in crime wasn't something she would tag along on. She said she hoped he would land on his feet someday, and marry an opera buff in the opera season. Stevo's passive resistance made his mother make a lamenting noise. Stevo decided his razzle dazzle sleeper spy career could be ended with a belly laugh. He knew it absurd that he would be anything but a laughing jackass.

After that flim-flam, long-winded laugh, Ektarina accepted the conclusion that her argument did help Stevo concentrate on a single idea that was his ambition. Able bodied work. He would whitewash what he had done, and tell no amusing stories. He could live in an amusement park if he wanted to, and never have to look over his shoulder and wait for the visitation of ghosts.

Tipene Stefaniya, the UN vote canvas representative maintained his companionship and friendship with Nevet and Tahvo. The inseparable twosome would gather and neck-tie boys for games and play, and gather then perfume girls to perform amusing pantomimes. Tipene was dangerously love sick for Steffie Toro, often seen modeling gowns for the bride's sister, who commanded everyone.

Now Estafania, named Zee, was brand new with her remarkable birth certificate. With this birth certificate you could buy a Fiance Visa to California/New York. You must have seen the requesting person, your fiancé within the last two years. Usually the persons marry as soon as possible during the first period of the Fiance Visa.

Stavros had made the most money off the boom of the camp. He was now mostly transacting daily business to rent space he had previously reserved for himself, or wiring funds, and certificates of bank notes. He was choosing a currency to denominate himself in. Etienne Isti, the bride's father had brought wealth, commerce, a tourist trade, and the start of a village that would become first a brick making factory. Within two years the brick factory would restore the streets and built rows and rows of housing. Near a hospital this part of the new city became the Spanish barrio

Nevet and Tahvo were experiencing communion after a friendship that was justified. Their in-tandem approach to looking the other way positioned them as impartial referees for prohibited amusement. These were the best two people imaginable as justices of the peace. Fashionable young people for want of anything better would take a free hand in teasing others, leave the café with the best dish of the day, wear saucy clothes, or get in the way and blunder into buffer zones where real preparations for the wedding might be taking place. They did not collapse, instead showed great open-mindedness.

Tahvo and Nevet were confidants and companions, as well as easy to get along with. They were enjoying the company of others. Tipene, who hobnobbed with them, could not stay off the subject of Steffie Toro. He constantly sought conversation with him about her. It also seemed Steffie Toro was everywhere. She would be seen modeling new gowns the color of a green frog, or a modest dress that was decorated with what looked like the flames of a roadster. She was hired by Ektarina Tomi as a chaperone to accompany Russian ladies, and men of the Railhead. These ladies and men went on a social fraternizations after the men's gifts and letters had won them the affections of their intimate companions. She was a close friend and crony of all the Russian ladies who were warned about men who liked to act like they were married without all the usual formalities. These familiar types would lunge forward seeking an embrace thinking they had been enticed to do so, but Steffie was the sidekick by the door who saw these passes as a stagger toward temptation brought on by the allure of a carrot. Foolishness sometimes brought on these displays. The covered entrance to the ladies tent was very well-lighted.

And Steffie was everywhere. Sometimes a cook, sometimes a fashion model, sometimes the hand-deliverer of a love note between Ateriasandre and Touma, a nurse who turned to a little boy's heartfelt cry, a decorator hanging a piece of fine art, an intellectual arguing appropriate behavior, and an escort holding the hand of newly arrived ostentatiously rich. She was also the subject of much gossip. Tipene Stefaniya heard so much about her he could not decide if being her formal companion to the upcoming wedding was so much the better, or so much the worse.

Estaban Dae, the current owner of Genius the lion, waited in his own private tent, and purchased and sold goods throughout the camp. Many times the bride's sister would come to him with a request for a special item, and Estaban would find, or send for that special element and see it fit into the exact place needed to light up the alluring spectacle of the wedding tent city. Every item the sister detailed was part of the story. Yet, even though he served the wedding family he had not set eyes on Ateriasandre y Teriasandre. He would sit motionless in the quiet of his tent and imagine her. Once he saw her shadow and her bold profile pass on the outside of her tent. But his incentive, his driving force was to serve her. To see her in person would set loose a free-for-all of euphoria.

Genius the lion, still on display in the tent city was considered the most gorgeous, manly male in the camp. He would stand princely in his cage and deliver a fine and fair beating to any man who thought himself more comely. Some people thought him a hallucination if they turned the corner to first find him in his lair. Anyone who approached his cage with pleasure noticed the telltale sign of the hang-dog wretched who would fade and leave behind a knotted tie, a rat's nest of twisted vest, or a murdered hat, clobbered by the dignified gaze of the macho Genius. If you came to rattle his cage, hair-stylists in the camp would later testify to your snarled and wispy head of hair.

Women approaching the cage would at first be hesitant and stammer, but their feelings would turn pendant with entertaining displays by Genius, of swami like everyday boy polishing of the eiderdown on his neck and stomach against the wooden bars of his cage. Ladies, despite the danger, felt no limitations and would poke, stroke, caress or rub his back as he walked close to the wooden bars. A stranger catching sight of this might set off a blood-curdling scream, but the lion would stare moving his jaws, and seem to chew out anyone not devil-may-care enough to be a wholehearted assistant. He held them in his gaze and drew from them a telltale sign. The lion was in the pink, and full of vim and vigor. He expected everyone to dispense generous bargains and bravery and stand near his stomping grounds.

His muscular tail was a weather vane of his emotions, and he would wave it at his admirers. Women would speak to him in whiskey voiced, and throaty tones. Men would chug-a-lug and wander around the outside of his cage like rovers, with enthusiasm, pleasure and delight. The haggard, and the hollow-cheeked would leave with a frazzled walk and return with statuesque and crackerjack female companions. This always seemed to usher in the discussion of the fur that he displayed on his neck that looked like an expensive collar and was the impeccable standard for chains, chokers or lavaliers in the camp. It was said everywhere that Genius the lion did inspire people's passions and was the bride's dowry to the people in the wedding tent city.

Ngongo, the keeper of Alisa the elephant, had placed himself in the position of being the largest casino operation in the camp. The game these two offered was Zener cards, the twenty-five-card deck that is used to rank a player's ability at ESP, extra sensory perception. There are five different cards in the deck, so with twenty-five cards, the odds of a player correctly predicting a card is twenty percent of the time. One out of five would be a normal equation for predicting the next card. A pair of dice will roll a lucky seven one out of six times, on the average. A Zener card will be predictably right one out of five times.

This game with Ndongo could be played on the back of Elisa in the howdah if the player wanted a private game and was willing to risk the hazard of being on the back of the elephant. This could make for exciting play, and a tour of the camp. This maneuver was soon the stepping stone that made a *dak* bungalow out of the seating on top of the elephant. Travelers and gamblers enjoyed the accommodations provided by Ndongo, on the back of Elisa. Once it was established he held dominion over gambling with Zener cards, was *rajah* and *wallah* of the spinning Zener cards, he hired an open space to display his game. At the beginning and at the end of each day he would teach interested ladies, sometimes Russian ladies, the *nautch*, a dance performed by girls. Then he would hire a *wallah* to pull the rope on the cloth ceiling fan he hung above the Zener card table. The ESP game was simple. Could you call the next card? What was your wager?

Alisa, the showboat elephant was all the while working around the camp, staying in the same fenced in pen, bathing regularly, and showing an increasing amount of intelligence. With her intelligence and ability to move freely about the camp when Ndongo elevated himself to bump and bulldozer work, Alisa was sneakily becoming a well-known thief. She could snatch cake and oval drinking bowls with her trunk, and empty them into her upraised mouth. She would raise and put on a pedestal cartons of melons, lettuce, and banana stalks then devour them one by one. She stole a beer keg and dropped it into the Zener tent. This left Ndongo tickled pink. She would raise ice containers with her truck and bathe herself in them. If this got on your nerves she could fill the air with a youthful shock by trumpeting her displeasure.

Ndongo's enthusiasm for his new game, and his fascination with betting the house, meant he sometimes turned his back on Alisa. That she stole a mattress, a weather vane, a tack-painting of dogs playing poker, a case of pan, the preparation of the betel palm leaf and lime juice for chewing, a case of buffalo milk butter and a silvery set of salt and pepper shakers. She was mischievous, spontaneous, would act off the cuff and on the spur of the moment. To some she was the life of the party. From others she got the cold shoulder.

The marriage was on tap now. You needed an introduction to the bride. How are you going to get this? Maybe the General can get it for you. An introduction that will allow you to provide a gold tooth for her husband and herself. This is a gift they are presumed to be going to accept, before the wedding ceremony. The male dowry, and the female dowry are being arranged. This is a traditional gift, but it is not polite to refuse it. Even if you think you don't need one. It is just a cap, but it's a fit for you. Showy. Seen when you eat cafeteria style. Gold at weddings. Then more gold, more weddings.

Estafania, the fiancé of Stavros, the eligible, generous and honorable cocoa shipper is intending to view the wedding from up close. She can get in the party if she had the right design for a formal Bedouin dress. Stavros had introduced Estafania to Etienne Isti, then they had a conversation with Ateriasandre and Touma, and they decided Stavros could get them the small amount of gold they needed, and then a dental assistant would make the teeth. Stavros sent a message toward the gold mine with some boys on motorbikes. They returned with the report the mine was abandoned. Stavros stacked cut lumber after that and Estafania went forward with her plan to find a tooth designer who would come make the teeth.

This was a smooth change in plan until Stavros realized Estafania was never one to abide by traditional rules. Then he watched Estafania make a mark on the wedding party, and private parties with investment ideas about the hospital and the community. They all bought a bunch of gold from her, at magnificent prices. It didn't come from the mine, but Stavros did act as broker in the transaction. He took a minor piece.

The teeth were easy. They came by the dozen, all wrapped in cotton and tissue. Teeth are fairly uniform, and can be made into models for gold caps. To give or get a gold tooth from someone is a danger. Then the danger will pass. People become prone to following the suggestions of others when wearing a gold tooth. They intend to show it off, and this can lead to toothsome displays of self-candling. Then you recognize a part of yourself is the actor with the gold tooth. If you have one so it is made to display, or you use one on a tooth. A gold tooth snug. The woman who'd displayed the gold teeth was careful to maintain her inventory. And observe where a gold cap was polished. You must be careful not to swallow it. Most were worth up to a month's pay. Others ten times less. A front cap. The gold teeth come in a box like a diamond ring. Or, a bottle. With cotton and plastic tweezers.

After that she sold shares in the gold mine. A real transaction. One hundred share documents. The local tax code allowed sale of their property right, expressed as local taxation rate. They sold certificates of ownership, and later would sell bonds based on the collection of fees, as the mine was going to explode with copper. The mine was a supplier and supplied copper and piping. The bonds only paid a percent that was high enough to generate interest, but the one hundred share certificates of mining participation had ownership bonuses, and paid double in royalty compared to the bonds. But they were negotiable and could go down in value. Face value. But they could go up with consideration to the mine as it is a high producing copper plant. They went up. Right now they might be completely worthless. They were cheap. One hundred shares. Nice paperwork. Estafania was paid a fee, a one-time collection for sale of these certificates. She sold many of them.

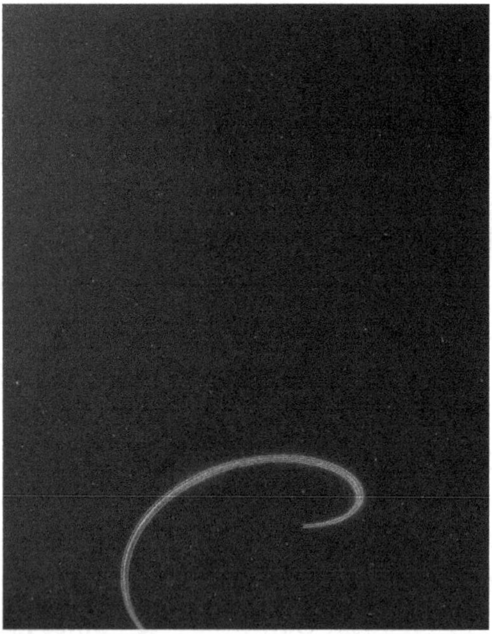

boomerang

Tin cupping is begging for money

Tin cupping, or Rhymin Bees N honey

CHAPTER SIXTEEN

Stavros said, "The way to keep the lion is to move his cage every day." Estaban was speaking to the phone. The lion moved because every day a wooden trailered crate as big as a two-story bedroom was available on a pallet. This was the most lucrative business. Short-term construction, and placement. Plus, the lion was a crowded arena, and the most that could be done was to dozer, then pick up waste. Bring in, then set down the house in the specified location. Detail the locking procedure.

What broke the wedding tent barrier was the sudden arrival of a sixty-person contingent from a large flat-bottom boat, and a small ferry. With escort privileges complete and escort to the private ceremony possible, the sixty-person contingent was the most direct connection since it was the home of host Etienne Isti. He who would on this night share a taxi with his wife on a trip to a retreat seventy miles distant. It was Etienne Isti who brought in a crate of pencil and ink illustrations and they were all signed Picasso. Like the big Picasso in Chicago. The one that is big enough to dance with a truck full of boulders. Etienne Isti brought on the bowing and the head kissing and the Egyptian ululation, again and again. Some were great to repeat themselves. Standing men crunched on small rocks on the edges of the singing and waited with poise. Etienne Isti having gifted the crowd with the pages of a Picasso notebook, hand delivered by the bomb squad escapee, who had returned with more sheets of good news, and a delivery laden with FedEx. The FedEx shared a taxi with everyone. This was the most convenient way to enter the tent with the most intimate bridal ceremony. By taxi. The bride's father was the one who stayed in the desert and overcame the environment and won his fortune, just buying concrete. With sixty came another sixty when the shipboard was down to its last man is the captain. So the line of dancers around the tent began to sway and come together at the ends. It would sway sensuously, and together. As it did a four-sided dance, then a circle came together. Two lines, two circles, one inside the other. The men and women facing each other and swaying in separate lines. In the midst of it all the wedding ceremony took place. Circles and lines were moving about and always the dancers were lining up for energetic dances with the other end of the swaying line. Four sides, the four lines in a square beside the wedding tent. Not a single woman would go home that night alone. The single and not married would chase tribes of children who might be harboring, or hiding an orphan. A bona fide adult responsibility. That is the indicator lite that went off in someone. A temporary auction, and the placement survivor is hoisted to an adult, and leaving under an adult's jurisdiction. Sale of the orphanage. Some went for a great price. Others went for lower accommodations.

The dancing spread out from the center, and different music was offered. This was customary, and necessary for the fifteen hundred persons within a half-mile of the tent. There was another three thousand within one mile.

Every boy and girl was taken home on that night. Sam went with a two hundred pound baker's assistant whose name was Bella. She lived near the river where the land was occasionally filled with hippos. Sam had the wherewithal to buy her a stove, and some flour, and she got a job in a hotel bakery. Then Sam moved from the hippos. No one knew or would have come to save him from Bella. His escape from Cardinal, was easier than an escape from Bella.

Singing engaged the entire wedding party and the lines of dancers, who congratulated the couple on their marriage. The pairing off was made by fate. This was destiny and had been for some time. Destiny brings congratulations and thanks. Poised for hand shaking, and head kissing.

Estafania ululated when nine flower bouquets arrived at the right moment. She paid for ten and got the tenth. Without hesitating when asked for the pleasure of dancing she stood and cried, then said yes, which meant lining up and swaying sensuously with the others. Love is being made between dancers and music. Even though the line stays connected there are constant comings and goings. The girls, all of them change partners looking for younger, faster, better-dressed men, and the men make fabulous impressions looking for younger, faster sessions and keep appearing on the stone with new partners, and a new step.

Farther away the dances are different. There is a Greek band playing. There are a few *cha chas.* A tall, tan lady in single strap heels, black clinging knit dress, cut open at the shoulders, and a fringed skirt that sways in the breeze. She is held by her bullfighter spurs to the ground. She spins a flat black hat.

A giant face arrives on a huge, flat, painted cover. It is the face of a bullfighter. It is held above the Spanish rumba being played by the Africans. Some were doing the tango. One pair was alone in the foxtrot. A simple one. These two have on matching shirts, pants, shoes, silver and red belts, big red hair, and silver earrings.

The jitterbugging was the furthest away, where there was cheek-to-cheek dancing. The two trumpets, saxophone, trombone, bass guitar, rhythm guitar, two drummers, organist, singer and twenty-five couples were enjoying the floor dances, and this public occasion for all of the dancers to show themselves.

All that was left was to unsplash the Bedouin princess. The palace train could be hers. Her mother and father had set out on their journey to a best friend's retreat.

This is when Sam came to Stavros with money, in Dutch gulders, and silver. Could the palace train of Ateriasandre y Teriasandre, and Touma Thomaz carry forty thousand silver gulders, to cover the import statements of an incoming train, on the coastal river, distant? Touma said he would deliver the money to the station ambassador, ticket agent. Sam was sending money and Touma would follow it.

Even the bride's sister was filled with envy when Teriasandre and Touma were on a honeymoon delivery task. The truth was that when taken to the other end of the financial arrangement, the store was being stolen. By the usual wholesale thief culprits. In plain view. The honeymooners had nothing to do with it. They were cautious about the delivery, and saw the result, lived through an injudicious tip-off, then observed and appreciated a retailer's dream for acquisition, expenditure, and turn around. High demand, low inventory. The train though pirated, was a useful acquisition. No trade ever goes for naught however, for the pirates stayed to drive the train, and Sam eventually gets a seacraft. Long story.

Touma and Teriasandre sat aboard the palace train car. They were no longer nervous. The bride price, and the male dowry had made all things into a bond and a marriage. They were happy and being carried along by passersby who are pushing the solitary car toward the station agent, who is waving a light behind them. There are three engines on this train. One at the front, one in the middle, and one at the end. The palace car is in the second section, behind the second engine. She has the furthest to go, to the coastal port.

Ixtaba, and Stevo Brakeman connect the hoses on the palace car. Both are wearing gold teeth. The bride and groom were sitting modestly on a couch in front of a viewing group of approximately one thousand persons. The windows on the car were open. Ateriasandre was dressed modestly but was flirting with the crowd, and gentlemen in it. She was famed for modesty but also famed for flirting. She was the most beautiful woman in the brilliantly illuminated car. It was quiet and the bride and her sister could talk through the open window about their health. They both appear in good health. The sister asks if she has poetry, but the other answers laughing and pounding herself on the chest, while the other looks on. Then the train starts to move. The sisters know how to say "Any day of the week" in many languages.

That is a code for them. Arabic. English, French, Spanish, Swahili, Italian, German, Dutch, Batuu, Russian. "Any day of the week." All of those spoken at Departure Road Station. The engineer often looks like a cockalorum, a small but self-important man. His primary function is to determine eligibility for workstaff and trade. Very demanding of straightforward and precise delivery.

As the train pulls away, Touma and Teriasandre, circle the porch of the car, waving, and dancing a two-step, holding the others' hands aloft. Then they wave with flowers in their hands, toss them to persons, then clutch fresh air to their breasts. They have fresh faces and turn old steps. Beside the train there is a band too close.

It is a noisy, Russian band with guitars, violin, bass fiddle, and singers. They all play the mandolin. They play Mozart and Beethoven. The band leader Tey claims one of them is a descendant of Genghis Khan, who invaded Russia in 1222 A.D. Tey says his great uncle was Galileo. They play loud music and bandy songs about the first recorded Olympic Games, in 776 B.C. Tey is an underground fancy name for tit for tat, the psychological warfare game.

Steffie Thom, and now Steffie Toro is enjoying the underground with Tey, the singer and bass fiddling nephew of Galileo. He is the new spy in town and his message is "baker, curl shraak after shraak onto the dome of the saj." The response is "She wore a mudraga and a headscarf."

An ending to spies. Overview spun his mudraga, and threw caution to the wind, gibbeting the story as it played out to the two Russians. Most of the instructions were saved from destruction. Save these instructions. Never attempt to override the safety feature.

Always unplug the device when not in use. Ce vetement n'offre acune protection contre le effets mecaniques, flames or other risks. Autres risques.

No place in the desert was clear due to winds and fires. A single in-flight fuel transfer at the border meant a nationwide vantage point from the plane. Where do you want to fuel after clearing this airspace? The landed in hail north of Las Vegas, so they lifted off soon after. A new heading then they landed in lightning in Area 51, which is where the tourists were. They stayed two days, at a campsite as Overview's report time was met at the hail strapped tower, and reporting for leave considered. The two Russian journalists were a hailstorm of new output in casing news and connected to an outside source at this point, cambie la orientacion o la, o la, ubicacion de la antenna receptora.

With the tin can, the camper as their base, the three stretched out a little behind the wheel of the vehicle. They drove to Salt Lake City, then drove to Reno, Tahoe, then camped in a bike trail parking lot, then headed back to Reno. Overview wanted to see a dance show with the big sign on the front of the casino, "Fatima by the Mountain." The show was a classic success in special effects and the song "Mountains High as Clouds" was sung to the Bedouin princess in the stage show. Chefo and Kiwini would have been glad to go to the show. But they were working on a terrain model in the trailer. Overview had shifted his plan to a desert location for a meeting with the pharmaceutical sales telephone callers. He and his two boogeymen had been buying per day fourteen thousand dollars' worth of pharmaceuticals. On a credit card. The pharmaceuticals were ditches as scored. They had bought more than an average clinic would use in three years. The ozadachennyy chelovek, doctors, were with Overview, the bugimen.

Most of the time the doctors looked up at the sky star gazing. Simple star gazing. There are places in the Silver State for excellent star gazing. A ghost town, Gold Point. In Belmont you can see sixty miles below from the head peak of the valley. Excellent star gazing. The two Russians stared at the sky.

This is the point where Overview realized what he wanted with a scale map of 1:150. One to One fifty. A map of difficult terrain. Could be streams and lakes. The related exercise is you must orient yourself within 250 feet of a point in a 1:50,000 map that shows start point and objective. One to fifty thousand. One foot on the map represents 50,000 feet on the terrain. It is a tactical exercise that means complete daylight land navigation. End is a secure halt area. In three hours' time. On foot.

What do you want to do? Surprise the team to the point on the map? No, I want to capture them. Or leave them in trouble at reaching their next objective. Disoriented. Weak in land navigation. It can happen to an intoxicated prince, can it not? It isn't really a game, as much as it is a tactical exercise that can lead to an unknown halt area. Something will be illuminated. Movement will show suspects on reconnaissance. On foot in daylight.

If a clandestine meeting is required Overview can set it up like The-Hole-in-the Wall Gang. Why not just do it in a reasonable place, by some buildings. With vehicles nearby, if you get scared. What if there is trouble from neighbors? What if the neighbors don't see this as a tactical engagement. You can't run up on the lawn yelling and scare somebody, "I want to load up on the meat in your freezer," and leave that alone. Overview began to think of the instructions. Conserve estas instrucciones. Conserve these instructions. Then the last. Turn off engine. Apaque el motor. He is beginning to see himself.

All of this to help his sister, and his niece. They were not able to control their own lives, because of someone, a phone caller, coming into their home. He had gone so far as to purchase over thirty thousand dollars worth of cases or cartons, in order that he could shake his credit card under their nose. He intended to pay, but only on terms that includes no more calls to his sister, or his niece. If he could get them to come to him, in the dark so he could silence them, make them respect his privacy, turn off the dismay of his sister and niece. What he represents to the callers he might not know. This he wants to do at the end of a difficult task, next to a wild goose chase. Chase down thirty thousand dollars on foot, by reading a 50,000 to 1 map. The fifteen minutes with the enemy he wanted on video, and witnessed by the two Russians. He wanted to scare somebody. Permanently. This sounds like a video game. But permanent in video games means you start at the previous level. Overview began a search of terrain in his target area. He began with a flight simulator. On computer. He wasn't backing down. He just wanted to look the possibilities over. The flight simulator stitched together a place that was like a theater with a stage exit. This began as a train trip that was meant to deliver chocolate. Then these ideas.

Flash identity, profit motives, proven methods, white collar professions, and all genders. Professions, writer, businessman, actor, servant, secretary, retiree. Lover, spouse, friend. The plane trip will not be a good representation of the reasonable man on earth.

Running out of luck in the world's biggest cattle yard is where this leads. Good thing you can get unobstructed views from what used to be the world's tallest building. Cattle yards are in Chicago, south of the Sears Tower. Now named Willis. 1973's advanced structure employed steel tubing designed into interlocking 75-foot squares. Design allowed large open spaces on the lower floors, with smaller floors on the above floors. All sides gave unobstructed views, of course. 1969's John Hancock Center was dwarfed by the 110 floors, of Sears Tower. That was the idea wasn't it. The 110 floors of the world's largest department store.

New York City in 1930 housed 850 feet of the tallest building in the world, the Chrysler building, with scalloped windows and a notable, lighted spire atop the cathedral of capitalism. Chrysler was the tallest for a year, or a year and a day, and the Empire State went higher with an antenna on top, in 1931.

Overview put on his light gray suit and considered and reconsidered an escapist attitude. The map and the plan both made you feel ready to fly. That's when Overview knew he was ready for a break.

Two bribed stops from there he was landing onboard a plane in Anchorage. I have spent a fortune in rubles. Ten thousand rubles is how much?

I spent one night at an expensive hotel, with double the rates for twin beds, a river water shower, and twice thin mattresses. At the airport I am switched from next Wednesday's flight, to today's leaving in two hours. I pay penalties in rubles but consider it a fabulous break. A Russian man appears calling my name saying my plane is about to leave. I make it through customs with personnel counting my money, then stamping my passport. Aboard the Alaska Airplane I meet bankers, and a Peace Corps member. After an interim stopover, first-class passengers move into second-class sections to balance the plane's "center of gravity." Just after takeoff we fly over handfuls of planes on the ground that will never fly again because of safety problems. We sing "Happy Birthday" to the pilot. After feeding the passengers, we are above Anchorage. I arrive with no reservation, no buses, no hotel and little hope. Have I run out of luck? Ninety-nine.

The best trip from Alaska, through Canada by water, to the state of Washington is called The Inside Passage. On a boat of any size or speed, this could take a few days or over a week. This is the most remarkable civilized backwater in the world. I have been sleeping on three chairs, under a full moon, to complete this trip. I imagine another trip, but one with only this destination in mind. Tomorrow is my last day of corn flakes, and blueberry muffins. There is where you can make friends. I meet kids. Then meet their parents. My philosophy, and doctorate degree help me interact with young kids, and parents. I have been promised a ride in a van because I have a single suitcase. My first grade friend agrees second grade is going to be tough, but not terrible, tough. Aboard the last stage ferry, deck seating has been struck, sleeping bags and tents rolled up, and the solarium swept. The van has a custom fit stowage area, behind the back seat. My suitcase is the right size. Solid land is yards away, and the ramp is solid.

UNSPLASH PHOTOGRAPHY CREDITS.

brian breeden **the palace train**
ruedi haberli **follow the sands to shifting sands**
carl-nenzen-loven **three undercover fledgling**
gregory buzdyk **by the train the girl and luggage**
hennie stander **a lady elephant walk**
robert thiemann **a genius lion**
james ballard **camels waiting to train in a chase**
patrick hendry **the bike turns in the best ending**
karima sitting **in the landscape a lady in fabric**
milad shams **lady in the mirror-as-Sitt-Fatima**
federico di dio **black sand on the mountain walk**
nicholas sampson **man on the mountain**
alan cornileu **look into the skylight**
roland losslein **on this train, on the trestle**
yash raut **the lady in the light as fireflies light**
marco mons **boomerang**
action vance **heaven and earth**
wolfgang hasselman **book cover**

READINGS

The Readings list reveals some names for excellent reading.
Some might be a chance to point to what is rare.
Others are exceptional for other reasons.
What has held out promise for me, I hold out to you. *stp.*

Bjork, Kenneth O. *West of the Great Divide, Norwegian Migration to the Pacific Coast*, Norwegian-American Historical Association, Lund Press, 1958, Minneapolis, MN.

Blackburn, Simon. *Oxford Dictionary of Philosophy*, 3rd Ed, Oxford University Press, 2016, Oxford, UK.

Brackenberry, Don. *Cowboy Poetry and Reminiscence*, Illustrated by Lon Hatch, Hungry Horse Publishing, 2005.

Broman, Mickey. *Nevada Ghost Town Trails*, Gem Guides Book Co., 1984, Baldwin Park, CA.

Catch 22, DVD, Hulu. Based on the novel by Joseph Heller. Paramount Television, 2019, Hollywood, CA.

Colman, Andrew M. *Oxford Dictionary of Psychology*, 4th Ed, Oxford University Press, Oxford, UK.

Complete Handbook of Pro Basketball, 1980 Season. Zander Hollander, Editor, Signet Books, 1979, New York, New York.

Destination Lake Tahoe, KC Publications, Las Vegas, Nevada.

Emerson, Connie. *The Cheapskate's Guide to Las Vegas*, Citadel Press, 1996, Secaucus, New Jersey.

Griswold, Rufus Wilmot. *The Republican Court or American Society in the Days of Washington*, D. Appleton & Co., 1854.

Illustrated Reverse Dictionary, The Reader's Digest Association, 1990, Pleasantville, New York.

Kane, Michael, Welder, Barbara, Cortes, Dalel. *Action Spanish for Law Enforcement*, Prentice Hall, 2002, Upper Saddle River, New Jersey.

Kennedy, Caroline, Editor. *A Patriot's Handbook*, Hyperion Books, 2003, New York, New York.

McCutcheon, Mark. *Roget's Super Thesaurus*, Writer's Digest Books, 1995, Cincinnati, Ohio.

Nevada Business. November 2020, Henderson, Nevada.

Nevada Historic Markers, Map & Index, Nevada National Bank, Bicentennial Edition.

Nevada's Valley of Fire, KC Publications, Las Vegas, Nevada.

Robb, Graham. *Balzac, A Biography*, Norton & Co., 1994, New York, New York.

Roberts, James A., Comptroller. *New York in the Revolution as Colony and State,* 2nd Ed., 1898.

Saglin, Jeffrey L. *Brother Desktop Publisher Owner's Manual*, AMACOM Books, 1989, Calabasas, California.

Should I Eat This, Consumer Reports, Expanded Third Edition, 2017, Yonkers, New York, NY.

Van Geldermalsen, Marguerite. *Married to a Bedouin*, Virago Press, 2009, London, UK.

Wetzel, Dan. *Jerry Tarkanian, Runnin' Rebel,* Sports Publishing, 2005, Champaign, IL.

heaven and earth

CPSIA information can be obtained
at www.ICGtesting.com
Printed in the USA
LVHW082328170422
716440LV00014BA/1019

9 781637 641262